THE YOUNGEST SPY

THE
Youngest Spy

Barry McDivitt

thistledown press

Library and Archives Canada Cataloguing in Publication

McDivitt, Barry, 1953-
The youngest spy / Barry McDivitt.

ISBN 978-1-897235-17-1

I. Title.
PS8625.D59Y69 2007 jC813'.6 C2007-901614-6

Cover: Detail from the original painting, *Confererate Christmas*
©1992 Mort Künstler, Inc
Cover and book design by Jackie Forrie
Printed and bound in Canada

Thistledown Press Ltd.
633 Main Street
Saskatoon, Saskatchewan, S7H 0J8
www.thistledownpress.com

Canada Council for the Arts | Conseil des Arts du Canada

Canadian Heritage | Patrimoine canadien

We acknowledge the support of the Canada Council for the Arts, the Saskatchewan Arts Board, and the Government of Canada through the Book Publishing Industry Development Program for our publishing program.

ACKNOWLEDGEMENTS

I would like to thank the following for their significant contributions:

Alison McDivitt
Johnson's Island Committee
R.P. MacIntyre, my editor

I am also indebted to the following authors whose works are treasure troves of information and insight about Canada during the Civil War: Greg Marquis, Adam Mayers, Robin W. Winks, Clayton Gray, John Headly, Oscar Kinchen and Fred Landon.

to Alison

One

(Excerpt of letter from Pvt. William Duguay. 11th Michigan Cavalry, June 6, 1863)

> *Dearest Lizzie:*
>
> *I fear the war is lost. Our commanders are fools, the soldiers are losing heart, and the enemy holds us in contempt. Many Americans are so tired of the war that they are demanding peace at any cost. I'd like to see the fighting end too. Then I can go home to Canada, where all is peaceful, and I'd be surrounded by the people I love . . .*

The words were those of a common soldier, composed after a bloody fight in a foreign field. Homesick and dispirited, it comforted him to think that at least his family was safe in Canada. Soldiers were encouraged to write home to prove they were still alive, so Private William Duguay wrote regularly. He tried to fill his letters with helpful hints to his son George about things like caring for chickens or mending a harness. It never occurred to him that the boy might need advice on how to control a panicked horse.

George Duguay held gamely to the reins, even though his arms felt as though they were in danger of being ripped out of their sockets. A gun blast had panicked the stallion, causing it to rear onto its hind legs. The boy kept his grip, even as he was lifted off the ground by the powerful animal. There was another sharp crack. The shooter was barely an arm's-length away. He was equipped with a modern revolver, allowing him to fire steadily. His target, a ragged saddle tramp, was running for his life. Each time the gun fired the noise caused the big mustang to buck. The horse's frantic dance nearly resulted in tragedy. The crazed beast dragged George into the line of fire. A bullet narrowly missed the youngster's head and plowed a gouge in the seat of the saddle. The gunman, surrounded by a foul cloud of gunpowder smoke, swore horribly at having his aim ruined.

Squealing in terror and outrage, the horse lashed out with a front leg, trying to free itself from George's desperate grasp. There was enough force behind the iron-shod hoof to crush a ribcage or split a skull open. George avoided death or serious injury by twisting his body as he hung from the horse. He'd sensed, rather than seen, the vicious kick. A flailing hoof grazed his side. Realizing that the boy had lost his footing, the stallion began to run. George was helpless. One of his wrists was entangled in the leather reins.

As the mustang stampeded down the dirt road, dragging George, they overtook the saddle tramp. The man was running a zigzag pattern in the hope it made him a difficult target. He veered into the animal's path and nearly suffered the indignity of being trampled by his own horse. At that moment George managed to shake himself free of the reins.

The tramp turned into an alley and disappeared. His attacker didn't attempt to follow. Instead he bellowed a threat. "Ah'll git ya, ya traitor!"

The frustrated gunman noticed the boy lying helpless in the street. He thought for a moment, frowned, and started walking towards the youngster. Then he spotted a piece of coloured paper fluttering in the light breeze. It had been torn from George's hand when the stallion bolted. The man bent over, reaching awkwardly, and picked up the paper.

"Confederate money." His tone was contemptuous. "He didn't even give ya a fair tip."

George found himself looking into the cruelest eyes he'd ever seen. He suddenly understood, with chilling clarity, that this man didn't intend to leave any witnesses behind.

"Sorry, son," said the gunman. "I know it ain't even your war." Then he squeezed the trigger. There was a loud click, but no explosion. Miraculously, George was still alive.

Even revolvers run out of ammunition. The stranger had emptied every chamber, firing at the saddle tramp. He cursed and fumbled in a pocket for more bullets. Shouted questions distracted him. People were pouring out of nearby buildings to see what all the excitement was about.

Gunfire wasn't often heard in the streets of Toronto in 1863. The young city on Lake Ontario already had a reputation for being rather quiet, dull even. So when bullets started flying, the citizens didn't know enough to keep their heads down, unlike their counterparts in American frontier towns. Instead, with an innocence that infuriated the shooter, they seemed determined to get a better look at what was going on. The gunman knew that somebody would soon get a good look at him, if they hadn't already, so he took to his heels. George was spared.

George Duguay was the last person you'd expect to end up in the middle of a gun-fight, even if his father was a soldier in the American army. He lived on a small farm on the outskirts of town and helped his mother look after several hundred chickens. Every morning he loaded baskets of eggs into a horse-drawn wagon and went into town to sell his wares.

The Pickford Inn was George's most important customer. It was clean and reasonably priced, which ensured that it was usually filled to capacity. The inn had a dining room that served dozens of breakfasts every day, so it needed a steady supply of fresh eggs.

That morning, as usual, George made a delivery to the Pickford Inn. Mary Eliza, a cheerful chambermaid about two years older, helped him carry the baskets of eggs. She was a terrible tease who'd made more than one young delivery boy blush. Her flirting and outrageous compliments never had the desired effect on George, to her profound disappointment. Instead of turning red or stammering he'd simply go about his work. Although she sometimes caught his intelligent eyes studying her, they never betrayed his thoughts. Mary Eliza couldn't tell if he was amused or offended by her comments. On that particular day she breathlessly told George that she thought she was falling in love with him. He never blinked, let alone blushed. Disappointed, Mary went off to clean rooms.

It was then that George was approached by a ragged man who asked for a favour. The stranger wasn't one of the Pickford Inn's typical guests. The inn attracted a higher class of customer and the shabby tramp looked out of place. He seemed to sense he didn't belong and was eager to leave. Furthermore, the man acted strangely. He paced nervously and kept peering out windows.

"If you fetch my horse and saddle it up, I'll pay you for your trouble," promised the outsider.

George often went to the nearby livery stable to retrieve horses for inn guests. They invariably tipped him a penny or two. He handed all the tips over to his mother, who had difficulty making ends meet most months. Without hesitation George agreed to run the errand. The fidgety tramp said he'd wait inside.

Shortly afterwards, upon returning with the saddled stallion, George was led to believe he'd hit the jackpot. The man slipped him a folded bill. The words One Dollar – Bank of Virginia were clearly visible at the top of the note. It was a magnificent tip. Still, it was an odd-looking bill. George had never seen anything like it. He unfolded it and looked closer. It was a Confederate dollar, which everyone knew was worthless.

George's face never betrayed his disappointment. He stoically held the horse steady while the deceitful stranger threw saddle bags over the animal's back. The tramp arranged the bags to his satisfaction, glanced up, and squealed in fright. He rudely pushed George out the way, reaching for the reins. The startled horse snorted and jumped backwards.

The cause of the commotion was a man who appeared out of nowhere. The instant he realized that he'd been spotted, the newcomer pulled out a pistol from under his coat and fired. It was done quickly, yet clumsily. The bullet slammed into the road instead of its intended target. The gun's roar sent the stallion into a panic. Instead of letting go of the reins and running for cover George instinctively tried to bring the horse under control, nearly losing his life as a result.

George was suffering from a split lip, a sprained wrist, numerous bruises and some pulled muscles. The injuries would have been much worse if it hadn't rained earlier in the day. The unpaved street had been transformed into a field of mud, dirty but soft.

A crowd of anxious people raced towards George. He struggled to sit up.

"Good heavens, it's the egg boy. Is he hurt?" The concerned voice belonged to Alan Pickle, owner of the Pickford Inn.

"His lip is cut and he's banged up pretty good," said Mary Eliza. "Thank heavens he wasn't shot."

The chambermaid noticed her friend's legs were shaky. She let him lean on her for support.

"What happened?" The question came from a tall, slim man with a prominent Adam's apple. His dark eyes darted around, taking in the scene. He acted like someone who was used to being in charge.

"Detective! You're exactly the man we need," said Pickle. "Someone just tried to shoot Alonzo Wolverton. I guess he wasn't fooling when he said he was being followed. Maybe we should have listened to him, even if he is a scoundrel."

"I was watching from the kitchen window," volunteered Mary Eliza. "Mr. Wolverton was about to get on his horse when a man walked up and started shooting. Poor George was dragged halfway down the street. The last I saw of Mr. Wolverton, he was running in that direction." She pointed.

"And he probably won't stop running until he hits Quebec City," Pickle said dryly.

The newcomer turned to George. "I want you tell me what happened?"

"Yes, sir. Are you really a detective?"

There was a moment's hesitation. "Yes, I am."

George was impressed. He'd never met such an important person before. Then, knowing it was his duty to help the authorities, he told the man everything he remembered about the shooting.

The detective seemed astonished by George's story. At one point he shot Pickle a questioning look.

"I'd say his information is probably accurate," said the inn's owner. "He's a reliable lad, not prone to exaggeration. George delivers eggs to us every day. He lives on a farm a few miles away. His father is fighting for the Union army."

Pickle had moved to Toronto from New York when he was a boy. He still had a lot of family in the United States and was a passionate Union supporter. The innkeeper reached over and gave the boy a pat on the head.

By the summer of 1863, the American Civil War had been raging for more than two years. The world watched in amazement as a great country split in two. The Southern States believed slavery was normal and that their prosperity depended on it. They resented the anti-slavery feeling that was growing in the North, so they separated and formed a new nation called the Confederate States of America. The remaining part of the United States had a bigger population and much more money than the rebellious South did. Despite those advantages, its armies had been defeated time after time.

In spite of its military successes, the Confederacy had some big problems. The economy was a disaster, its money was worthless, and casualties had been so high that it was running out of men. Unless something dramatic happened soon, the South was doomed to fail.

The detective beamed in delight and shook George's hand. "I'm honoured to meet a supporter of our cause," he said.

George remained silent, not knowing what to say. He always found it difficult to explain why his father was fighting a war in a foreign nation. Luckily he wasn't expected to respond.

"Peelers are coming!" a man cried in warning. He'd used a slang word for police that had recently spread to Canada from England.

"I'd best be going then," said the detective. "I don't want it to look like I'm interfering with the investigation. You know how prickly the Canadians can get." He disappeared down the same alley that had provided an escape route for the gunman.

A young policeman trotted up. His uniform was stained with mud. "I understand there's been a shooting," he said excitedly.

He was a new recruit and this was the most interesting thing that had happened since he'd joined the force. Previously he'd spent most of his time chasing Toronto's bootleggers, who were notorious for selling alcohol to children.

"No one is to leave the scene," ordered the constable. "Inspector Stansbury will be here in a few moments. He will wish to question each of you."

"Stansbury is a hard case," muttered Pickle to a swarthy man standing next to him. "And he's certainly no friend of ours."

"Southern sympathizer?" asked the man in a whisper.

The innkeeper scowled and nodded.

Inspector Stanley Stansbury looked very much like the British military officer he'd once been. His back was straight, his hair and moustache were neatly trimmed, and he had a gruff manner that had caused many young army recruits to tremble in fear. He was accompanied by a burly, younger man.

"I hear your friends have been acting up, Pickle." The inspector was in a fury. He strode to where the nervous innkeeper was standing. "Isn't it amazing that there's a gunfight outside your establishment just a few days after a bunch of American agents move in. Trying to bring the war a little closer to home, eh?"

Stammering, Pickle began to argue that he had no idea what might have caused the fight. Stansbury cut him short.

"There has just been an attempted murder outside your inn," snapped the inspector. "I presume it's related to the ongoing civil war in your country of birth."

A youthful voice piped up. "I'm quite sure you're right, sir."

Stansbury blinked in amazement and stopped his rant. He wasn't used to being interrupted. The inspector glared at the dirty, bloody-faced boy who had spoken.

If George was unnerved by Stansbury's piercing stare it didn't show. He continued with his story. "The gunman shouted 'traitor' at the man he attempted to kill."

"Traitor, eh? That certainly sounds like something that soldiers, rather than common criminals, would yell at each other."

The comment came from Stansbury's companion. Unlike his boss, Detective Colin Campbell had been born in Canada. His manner was casual and his clothes were sometimes sloppy, traits that did not endear him to the inspector.

"It's obvious the attacker was a Confederate and the intended victim was a Yankee," declared Stansbury confidently.

George spoke up again. "Actually, it sounded to me like both men had Southern accents. And the one who nearly got shot and ran away was carrying Confederate money." He handed over the muddy bill.

"Isn't that interesting," said Detective Campbell in a quiet voice. "A Southerner visits a Toronto hotel that is being used as a base by Northern agents. Then someone tries to kill him. Which side wants him dead, the Confederates or the Americans? Maybe he managed to betray both sides. I understand that happens a lot in this war."

He looked at Pickle. The sullen innkeeper kept mum, refusing to volunteer any information.

Stansbury decided it was time to interview George privately. He led the boy to the other side of the street. Campbell stayed behind to question Pickle and the others.

"What's your name, boy?" Stansbury spoke harshly. He was deliberately attempting to intimidate the youngster and let him know who was boss. The bluster didn't have its desired effect though. George didn't even blink as he met the inspector's glare.

"My name is George Duguay, sir. My father is away at the war. I help my mother on the farm. Every day I come into town to sell eggs. Mr. Pickle is one of my best customers."

Stansbury noticed that the boy wasn't reluctant to talk. In fact, he readily volunteered information that hadn't been asked for.

"I already told all this to the other detective, sir," George added politely.

The inspector blinked in surprise. "Other detective? Who in the blazes are you talking about?"

"I didn't get his name. He seems to be a friend of Mr. Pickle."

George described the man who'd interviewed him. By the time the boy had finished, Stansbury was livid.

"That's Will Bullock, I'm sure of it. Benson, his partner, is standing over there. He's the blond chap wearing the blue jacket. How dare they interfere in my investigation."

George couldn't understand why the inspector was so annoyed. "Is something wrong?" he asked. "Aren't they really detectives?"

"Oh they are certainly detectives," said Stansbury grimly. "The problem is that they're American. That inn you deliver eggs to has become a nest of Yankee spies. The Americans want to keep an eye on all of the Confederate agents that have suddenly infested this mud-hole that you colonials pretend is a city."

George was astonished. "Why are Confederates and Americans spying on each other in Toronto?" he asked. "What do we have to do with them?"

Stansbury wouldn't have bothered to reply to a mere boy, even if he'd known the answer.

Two

(Excerpt of letter from Pvt. William Duguay. 11th Michigan Cavalry)

My Dearest Lizzie:

Some American newspapers are calling for war with England. They say the Confederacy couldn't continue to fight if it weren't for all the supplies and weapons the British sell them. There is talk of invading Canada to capture it from the British. I can't imagine anything more terrible than being sent to fight my own people . . .

Canadians were fascinated by the bloody war that was tearing apart their American neighbour. They wagered money on their favourite army, just as they would bet on a horse race or wrestling match. The newspapers were full of stories about the latest campaigns and battles. Men who had never ever fired a musket felt qualified to debate tactics and explain their theories as to why large, well-equipped Yankee armies were regularly whipped by their ragged foes.

The Confederates seemed to be blessed with better generals and a remarkable fighting spirit. Those same Southerners also had a reputation of being polite and likeable. Why, it was almost as if they were Canadians.

Americans, on the other hand, were generally portrayed as pushy and money-hungry. It was also widely believed that the United States was determined to steal all of Britain's colonies in North America. From Nova Scotia to Upper Canada many people delighted at news of yet another Rebel victory. Ten thousand Canadians actually put on grey uniforms and fought for the Confederacy.

Despite the widespread suspicion of America, the Union cause received even stronger support. The war was seen by most Canadians as a noble struggle to free the slaves. Slavery had been abolished throughout the British Empire many years earlier. Thousands of escaped slaves had made it to Canada, helped by a secret group of sympathizers known as the Underground Railway. Newspapers often carried stories of the hardships suffered by the runaway slaves on their journey north.

Forty thousand Canadians joined the Union forces. Some of the men were simply looking for adventure. Others considered the war a crusade against slavery. Many, perhaps most, did it for the money.

The American army had suffered huge casualties and was desperate for men. The US Government began offering a bounty to every man who volunteered. The bounty was more than many ordinary workers earned in two or three years of honest labour. The money was very tempting, especially to a poor man.

George loved the fact his family finally had property of its own. Before this, he'd lived his life on a farm owned by an absentee landlord. William Duguay, George's father, was a tenant farmer who did all the work while the landlord took most of the profit. There was no point in complaining. The landowner was a harsh man who had the right to kick his tenants off the farm for any reason. The Duguays could starve to death for all he'd care.

Like most other poor men William Duguay dreamed of owning his own land. Although he worked hard he earned so little that it was almost impossible to save any money. One of the neighbouring farms was owned by an elderly Dutch bachelor who raised chickens. He'd died the previous summer, leaving his property to a nephew in Holland. The young man had no interest in his inheritance, other than what it might be worth, so he put it up for sale. The price was very reasonable and William Duguay desperately wanted to buy the farm. Unfortunately he didn't have any money.

Duguay knew of only one way that an honest man could quickly get his hands on a thick wad of cash. He joined the Union army. The United States government paid him a two hundred dollar bounty. With that money, along with a loan from the bank, Duguay was able to buy the farm. Looking after chickens takes time, but the work isn't hard. William figured his wife and son would be able to run the farm until he returned from the war.

"The boy is sharp," said Detective Campbell. He deliberately leaned against the office wall, knowing it annoyed the Englishman.

Inspector Stansbury simply grunted, which was his way of saying he hadn't made up his mind yet. He scowled at the sight of the slouching Canadian. When Stansbury stood or sat his back was always perfectly straight, just the way he'd been taught in the army. It bothered him when others seemed too relaxed. He thought it made them look sloppy.

"I wonder if the gunman really was shooting with his wrong hand?" continued Campbell.

"It would certainly help explain why he missed," admitted Stansbury. "Most Americans seem to be very handy with firearms. Yet that one fired six times at fairly close range and didn't score a single hit."

During his interview with the police, George had mentioned that he thought the bushwhacker wouldn't normally have held a gun in his right hand.

"How in thunder could you possibly know that?" Stansbury had snapped.

"Because his arm was all jerky," replied George evenly. "I'm left-handed, so I've had to learn how to do things with the weak hand." He held up his right hand. "This gets pretty shaky when I try to do things with it for the first few times. When the man pulled out his cavalry pistol, he was having trouble handling it. It made me think of how I must look to others. I don't think he's had as much practice using his right hand as I've had."

Being left-handed was considered a very bad habit. George's parents and teachers had worked hard to 'correct' him. Sometimes his left hand had even been tied behind his back, forcing him to use the right hand for writing or doing simple chores. For George it had been pure torture. It had also left him with deep sympathy for anyone else who was being forced to use a hand that didn't always work the way you wanted it to.

Now, hours after the interview, Detective Campbell was still thinking about what the boy had said.

"Why would someone shoot a gun with their wrong hand?" Campbell asked. Then he answered his own question. "It would make sense if his stronger arm had been injured or wounded."

The detective took a pistol from his desk drawer and tucked it into his belt. Then he stood up and pulled it out as quickly as he could with his left hand. The barrel got caught in his belt. Campbell gave the gun a hard yank, freed it, and then pointed it at an imaginary enemy.

"That wasn't very smooth, or fast," he admitted. "I can't imagine my aim would be any good, even if I was sporting a cavalry pistol."

The last comment was a sly dig at the Englishman. George had identified the shooter's weapon as a modern cavalry pistol. Stansbury expressed doubt that a simple farm boy could properly identify such a weapon. George insisted he was right. Hanging from a wall at home was a recent photograph of his father. In the picture William Duguay wore the uniform of a Michigan cavalry regiment and held a long-barrelled pistol. The inspector listened to the description of the gun and reluctantly conceded the boy knew what he was talking about.

The two men were quiet for a while, each thinking their own gloomy thoughts. Stansbury thought about how much he disliked being in a colonial backwater like Upper Canada. He'd only recently arrived from England. His job was to make sure the Americans and Confederates behaved themselves while they were on British territory. As if that weren't difficult enough, all he had for help was a handful of Canadian police officers. They had their own way of doing things and resented working for an outsider.

The inspector was the first to break the silence. "There are far too many Confederates in Toronto right now," he said. "More of their agents and supporters arrive every day. They claim they're only here to buy supplies for the war effort and help escaped prisoners get home. I don't believe it for a moment."

"The Americans don't believe it either," replied Campbell. "That's why they're sending their own agents here. To keep an eye on the Rebels."

"And now the two sides have started shooting at each other on the streets of Toronto," complained Stansbury. "If we allow it, they'll probably end up having a full-scale battle."

"Perhaps we should express our concerns to both sides tomorrow," suggested Campbell.

"That's exactly what I was thinking," said Stansbury. "We'll politely ask them to behave themselves while they're enjoying our hospitality."

Actually, he had no intention of being polite.

Lizzie Duguay was outraged. "How dare the Americans and the Confederates do their dirty work in our country," she huffed. "Innocent children could end up dead. I had no idea that all this spying was going on."

She dabbed at her son's bruised lip with a cloth.

George was proud of his newfound knowledge. "The Confederates have been staying at the Royal Roads Hotel for months. Now a bunch of Union agents have moved into the Pickford Inn."

"What are they up to?" asked Lizzie.

George realized that, for the first time in his life, he possessed inside information. It left him with a delicious sense of power. He got up from the chair and stretched. Nearly every muscle was throbbing. George knew his badly bruised body was going to feel even worse in the morning.

"I don't think anybody really knows what all the spies are up to, but those two detectives intend to find out," said George.

"They seem to be very worried." He'd already told his mother all about Stansbury and Campbell.

Lizzie got her son another piece of bread and bacon fat and coaxed him into sitting down again. Her eyes darted to the photograph of a soldier hanging on the wall. The man's face was stern, which was the fashion of the day. Nobody ever smiled when they were doing something as important and expensive as posing for a photographer. The absence of a smile bothered Lizzie. In real life William Duguay was a cheerful man who always had a grin on his face. There was something else about the photograph that troubled her. Her husband was wearing the uniform of the enemy.

The spy walked through the evening downpour, grateful that the miserable weather was keeping almost everyone indoors. For this type of business the fewer people around the better.

Toronto's waterfront was larger than he'd thought it would be. The docks were crowded with steamers and sailing ships. If the vessel had a Union Jack on its flagpole he passed by with barely a second glance. However, if the ship were flying the Stars and Stripes the spy would stop and study it carefully.

By the time his mission was completed the man was cold, wet and hungry. Just a few blocks away, in a fine hotel, a number of his countrymen were living luxuriously. The secret agent did not plan on joining them at the supper table. In fact, he hoped they didn't even know he was in town. As far as he was concerned they were incompetent amateurs who were wasting precious time and money.

The spy knew his country was in grave peril. He'd recently met with some very important men in his national capital. They felt his plan was extremely risky, but they'd approved it just the same. If it worked it would change the map of North America.

Three

(Excerpt of letter from Pvt. William Duguay. 11th Michigan Cavalry)

Dearest Lizzie:

I have sad news. One of my best friends in the regiment was kicked in the head by a horse and died. I believe I'd mentioned John Klassen to you in some of my earlier letters. He should have been in the infantry instead of the cavalry, as I never met a man who had more trouble with horses.

We still haven't been paid and I am flat broke. I will have to borrow the money to mail this . . .

"Can the egg boy be trusted?"

The answer was of the utmost importance to Will Bullock. He was in charge of all the American secret agents in Toronto. The detective had been the first one to talk to George after the shooting. The youngster's calm intelligence had impressed him.

"I suppose George is reliable," said Alan Pickle, shrugging. He shifted uncomfortably in his chair. The old leather cushion had split open and the stuffing was spilling out. Pickle pulled out some black fleece and examined it curiously.

The detective realized that Pickle was trying to figure out what sort of material the cushion had been stuffed with.

"That's Negro hair. Plantation owners sheer their slaves like sheep and sell the hair to make cushions and mattresses. It's supposed to be softer than horsehair. My guess is that your chairs were made somewhere in the Confederate States."

Pickle frowned and dropped the hair to the floor. Mary Eliza could sweep it up later. He turned towards his very important guest and tried to pay attention to what was being said.

The innkeeper hadn't visited the United States since he was a teenager, but he was a strong defender of the Union cause. He often spoke of the glory of battle and expressed regrets about being too old to serve in the American army. However, as even his own family said it is easy to be heroic when the nearest battlefield is hundreds of miles away.

Now, after the shooting in his front yard, the war was much too close for comfort. Pickle simply didn't have the stomach for gunplay. The realization came as quite a shock. He'd always imagined himself as being brave.

"You told us the boy's father is fighting in the Union army," continued the detective. "So it stands to reason he's well disposed towards our cause." He noticed that his host was in a nervous funk and assumed it was because of the shooting.

"Why are you so interested in a country bumpkin who delivers eggs?" asked Pickle, a little testily. He liked George, but didn't think the boy was anything special.

"We will occasionally need someone to hand-deliver correspondence for us," said Bullock. "Nobody pays the slightest attention to local delivery boys as they go from one place to another. That's why they're perfect messengers."

"George hasn't got much education, but he's certainly capable of performing simple chores," admitted Pickle. "He knows his way around the city and he's very conscientious. Look, here he is now."

The two men glanced through the dining room window as an open carriage pulled up to the inn. The morning's shipment of eggs had just arrived.

Every day, well before it got light, George and his mother went into the hen houses and collected eggs. There were usually well over two hundred a day in the summer, considerably fewer in the winter. The eggs were carefully placed in baskets filled with straw. That way they wouldn't break during the journey over rough roads into town.

George's best customers were hotels and boarding houses. They often took all the eggs he had. If there were any left over George would go from door to door, offering his wares to housewives. It never took him very long to sell out. Then he would drive back to the farm and do the rest of his chores.

The family relied on an elderly gelding for transportation. Winchester willingly allowed himself to be harnessed to a buckboard or ridden bareback. He knew the daily route so well that George occasionally napped during the four-mile trip from the farm into the city.

"Hello, handsome. I think that split lip and all those bruises make you look a hero returning from the battlefield." Mary Eliza, the Pickford Inn's chambermaid, was teasing again.

Once again she was disappointed by the lack of a response. George didn't show any sign of being pleased or embarrassed by her comments. He nodded affably, as if she'd just made an innocent comment about the weather, and got on with his work.

Mary Eliza had been raised in terrible poverty in Liverpool, England. By the time she was ten, her family could no longer afford to feed her. The British government often sent poor children to its far-flung colonies to work as servants or farm labourers. Mary made the long sea journey to Upper Canada on a foul and overcrowded sailing ship.

Many child immigrants were abused and overworked by their employers, but Mary Eliza was reasonably lucky. Although Mr. Pickford wasn't a warm-hearted man, he wasn't cruel either. As long as the girl did her job properly she was pretty much left alone. She had her own mattress in a storage room, decent food, and half a day off every Sunday. Life was much better than it had been back in Liverpool. Free from hunger, dressed in clean clothes, Mary Eliza was blossoming into a happy and clever girl. She even seemed to enjoy her menial job.

Mary Eliza was notoriously flirtatious and it was commonly believed she was already looking for a husband. She was certainly paying a lot of attention to some of the American gentlemen who had recently arrived at the inn.

"Let me help you with those eggs," volunteered the girl. There was a mischievous glint in her eyes. "That basket looks very heavy. I'm sure you're feeling weak after yesterday."

George finally rewarded Mary Eliza's persistence with a grin. He could have easily held up the basket with a single finger. Despite his protests, the girl insisted on carrying the eggs into the kitchen for him.

Mrs. Pickle was standing beside the enormous wood stove stirring a pot of stew. The stew would simmer all day. She was a very quiet woman who always seemed to be sick.

Mrs. Pickle looked up from her cooking duties as the two young people entered the room. She put down her spoon and took the basket of eggs. Then the woman carefully counted out a few coins and handed them to George. When she'd finished she said, "One of our guests would like to see you for a minute. He's sitting with my husband in the dining room. You can go in there now." It was an order, not a request.

George had never been in the dining room before. He was very impressed with what he saw. The wallpaper was a deep purple. George didn't even know that such a colour existed. He was used to living in a plain log cabin that didn't have any paint, inside or out.

The furniture struck him as being remarkably luxurious. The tables had ornately carved legs and the chairs actually had leather red cushions on them. George was used to the simplest of furnishings and had never sat on a cushioned seat.

It was just before breakfast so most of the tables were empty. In fact, the only people in the dining room were Pickle and another man.

"Hi, George," said the man, smiling. "Do you remember me?"

"Yes, sir. You're Mr. Bullock, the American detective."

"That's right. I want to tell you how impressed I am with the accuracy of the information you gave me yesterday. I've met trained police officers who couldn't do as well."

"Thank you, sir," said George. He sensed the man had a lot more to say.

Detective Bullock studied George between sips of coffee. The boy had a trustworthy face, although it didn't show much emotion. "I understand your father has joined the American army."

"Yes, sir. He's in the cavalry."

Bullock took an envelope from his vest pocket and placed it on the table. "Your father is fighting for a noble cause, as I'm sure you know."

"He's helping free the slaves," said George proudly.

"Well . . . yes, that too," said Bullock, frowning slightly. He didn't particularly care if the slaves were ever freed or not. To him the war was about preserving the United States. "Anyway, I was hoping you'd be able to do me a favour once in a while."

George readily agreed. He was always ready to run errands in return for a few extra cents.

"Do you know where Frank LaSalle's barber shop is?" asked Bullock.

"Sure, I go past it almost every day," said George."

"Perfect. I'd like you to take this envelope to him. He'll probably tell you to wait for a little while. Then he might ask you to bring another message to me. Oh, and one more thing. Make sure you bring a dozen eggs with you when you go into the barbershop. You'll be paid for the eggs, of course."

Although it sounded odd to George, he nodded his head in agreement.

Bullock handed the boy fifty cents. "This should pay for your eggs and your time."

George was astonished, and for once it showed. The money was more than he'd normally earn from running errands in a whole month. He stared at the two coins in his hand.

The detective saw the look of disbelief on the boy's face and misinterpreted it. "It's American money," he said. "I hope that's okay."

"Oh, that's just fine," George assured him. There was a terrible shortage of coins in Upper Canada. American money was readily accepted everywhere.

George arrived at Frank LaSalle's barbershop just after it opened. The boy remembered Detective Bullock's instructions about bringing some eggs with him, although he had no idea why he was supposed to do so. He had no experience in the ways of spies.

Bullock had wanted his young messenger to look perfectly normal to any Canadian or Confederate agents that might be keeping an eye on the barbershop. They'd think it strange if an egg boy wasn't carrying any eggs with him when he made a delivery.

The barber was a short, chubby man who watched George intently as he entered the shop.

"Are you Mr. LaSalle?" asked George.

"Yes, I am."

"This is for you," said George as he carefully handed over the letter. Then he held up his basket. "The eggs are for you too."

The barber's eyes narrowed as he looked at the envelope. He tucked the letter into his apron and walked to the window. After checking to see if anybody suspicious was outside he turned to the messenger.

"Stay right here," he said to George. Then he opened a door at the rear of the shop and went into a room. A moment later he was back.

"Can you wait for a little while?" asked the barber. He seemed friendly.

George politely said, "Yes, sir," and moved towards a chair.

"That hair of yours is getting a little long," noted LaSalle. He looked at the boy with professional interest.

"That's what ma says," agreed George. "She was telling me just this morning that it's about time to get the scissors out."

"Well, I don't mean to be critical of your mother," said the barber. "But I know I do a better job than she does. I don't have any customers yet, and we have time to kill, so let me give you a cut. We'll call it payment for those eggs you brought in. My missus will be delighted to get them."

George was so surprised by the offer that he hardly knew what to say. He'd never had his hair cut by a professional. In fact, nobody he knew had ever been to a barber before. Almost everybody, except for city folk with spare cash, depended on family or friends to cut their hair.

"C'mon, sit down," said LaSalle, pointing to his barber's chair.

George relished the thought of having a new experience. He hurried to obey.

The barber was very good. He didn't even have to put a bowl over George's head to use as a guide, the way his mother did. When he'd finished LaSalle picked up a mirror to show off his work to George. It was the first time in his life the boy had actually seen the back of his own head.

There was a knock on the back door. LaSalle quickly put down his scissors and left the room. He returned almost instantly and handed a different envelope to George.

"Take this to Bullock," said LaSalle. "Make sure you don't give it to anyone else but him."

"I'll bring it straight to him," said George obediently.

"No!" said the barber sharply. "That might look suspicious. Complete your deliveries. Then stop at the Pickford Inn on your way back. Don't rush in to deliver the letter. Take your time. Give your horse some water or go to the outhouse. Then you can go in and make your delivery."

Thoroughly confused, George nodded and went outside.

Despite the rumble in his stomach, the spy was a contented man. Two newspapers were folded neatly on the bed in his shabby room. One of the papers was from New York City. Most of the articles were about how badly the war was going for the United States. The Union army had been thrashed time and time again. The soldiers complained that they'd fought bravely, but that incompetent generals had let them down. The men were becoming dispirited and homesick. Recently they'd started deserting by the thousands.

There was also an article complaining about the severe losses that American merchant ships were suffering at the hands of Confederate raiders. Most of the Rebel warships were built in England, a fact that infuriated the US government.

Earlier in the war an American frigate had stopped and searched a British merchant vessel. Two Confederate diplomats who'd been travelling to Europe were arrested. Britain ruled the waves and did not allow any other nation to seize passengers from her ships. The Royal Navy was ordered to prepare for war against the United States. Eventually the Americans backed down and released the captives. However, tensions between the two nations remained high.

The other newspaper that the spy had read with great interest was *The Times of London*. It reported that more British troops were on their way to defend Canada from a possible American invasion.

As far as the spy was concerned, the news couldn't have been more promising. He moved from his chair and gazed out of the window of his second-storey room. On the street below, a boy was getting out a buckboard. In one hand was a basket of eggs. The spy's stomach growled again.

Four

(Excerpt of letter from Pvt. William Duguay. 11th Michigan Cavalry)

Dear Lizzie:

The Union generals have no idea how to use cavalry properly. All we do is guard supply wagons. We should be raiding deep into enemy territory, the way the Rebels do.

I'm sending you 20 dollars, which is half of what the army owed me. I hope to get the rest soon. Use the money as you see fit. I'm glad the farm is doing well. George has always been a good worker . . .

"Are these eggs fresh? I'm sure they're not!" The wrinkled old woman picked one up of the eggs and studied it suspiciously.

George sighed. It was like this every time he visited Mrs. Olsten. She was unpleasant to deal with and never wanted to pay a fair price. He only called on her if he hadn't been able to sell all of his wares elsewhere. The Olsten boarding house was a large two-storey structure that had been sadly neglected. The paint was peeling and the front porch sagged dangerously. A skinny goat was permanently tied up in the front yard to keep the weeds down.

"The eggs are fresh this morning," he assured her. "If you keep them in a cool place they'll stay good for a week." Eggs don't spoil as quickly as most other foods, which made them popular at a time when there was no refrigeration.

Suspicious as always, Mrs. Olsten held up an egg and carefully checked it for cracks. She always inspected every single one.

"I'll give you a penny for the lot of them," she finally declared.

"Three cents," said George. "It's the same price everybody else pays."

"You're a cheat!" complained the woman. "I can get bigger and fresher eggs than these at the market for a penny."

Her claim was false, as they both knew. On most days they would have bargained for a while and then George would reluctantly agree to take two cents.

Today was different. George had earned fifty cents in tips and was feeling rich and cocky. He shook his head firmly and put the basket in the back of the buckboard. Mrs. Olsten watched in horror. The boy had gained some self-confidence since she'd last seen him. She didn't like it one bit.

"I'll buy the eggs," said a man as he walked out of the boarding house. He was tall with sandy hair and a neatly-trimmed moustache. His clothes looked expensive, which was very unusual for the sort of person who usually stayed at such a run-down facility.

Outraged, Mrs. Olsten turned to the man. "This is no concern of yours," she snapped.

"It is if I want a full stomach," replied the man. His voice was soft and he drawled his words. "I regret to say, ma'am, that

I've found the rations rather skimpy at your establishment. If I stayed here much longer I'm sure I'd become as skinny as that poor goat."

George wasn't surprised by what the man said. He'd heard that Mrs. Olsten served small portions to her boarders.

"And what do you think you'll do with the eggs if you buy them?" said the old woman sharply. Her eyes flashed in triumph. "There's no way I'll be cooking them for you. And don't think you can go into my kitchen and fix them yourself."

"I think I might be able to help the gentleman out," said George.

From under the seat of the buckboard he took out a small sack. Every morning his mother gave him some hard-boiled eggs. He was usually able to sell them to labourers who wanted a snack or to travellers setting out on a journey. The ones that weren't sold became part of George's lunch.

"I've got four left," he said. "My ma boiled them up this morning."

"I don't care what the cost is," said the man, grinning. "I'll take them all."

Mrs. Olsten was furious. "Both of you get out of here," she yelled. "I won't have my cooking criticized by an ignorant brat and an ill-mannered Yank."

Her guest grimaced. Being called a Yank clearly caused him pain. "The truth is, ma'am, that I was planning to look for new quarters anyway. I'm afraid your establishment has proved to be a disappointment."

He handed her some money. "I believe his will more than cover what I owe you. Now, if you'll excuse me, I'll just run upstairs and grab my bags."

George had been listening carefully to the man, paying special attention to his accent. He knew the landlady had been badly mistaken when she called her guest a Yankee.

A chill ran down George's spine. A thought had just occurred to him. Somewhat to his surprise he heard his own voice say, "Will you be moving to the Royal Roads, sir?"

The man froze and turned to George. He looked at the boy keenly. "Why do you ask that?"

"That's where most Southern gentlemen stay when they visit Toronto, sir," replied George. His face was a mask of innocence.

Although the spy didn't lose his composure he was fuming inside. The Confederate spy ring at the Royal Roads was supposed to be a secret. So why did everybody in Toronto seem to know about it? He was more determined than ever to keep away from the hotel.

"I'm afraid I don't know anybody who is staying at the establishment you mentioned," said the stranger.

Despite the denial, George was certain he'd guessed correctly. The accent originated in the southern part of the United States.

George had become bolder as a result of his recent adventures. In the past, he simply would have said a respectful goodbye and headed off to complete his chores. Now, for some reason he couldn't explain, he desperately wanted to find out more about the stranger.

"I know where there's a fine boarding house, if you prefer them to hotels," volunteered George.

The man stared at him for a long moment. Then he smiled. "Is it near here?" he asked.

"Not too far, sir. Mrs. Macdonald runs it. I bring eggs there every morning. Today she mentioned that one of her lodgers has moved out. I'm sure the room is still available. I've heard she feeds her guests very well."

"That certainly sounds promising. Could you direct me to her house?"

"I can give you a ride if you'd like," said George. "It isn't out of my way."

"That is very kind of you," said the man. "It won't take me long to pack. I'll return in a moment."

"Well I won't need as many eggs now that he's going," said Mrs. Olsten grumpily. George had forgotten she was still there.

"Tell you what," she said. "I'll give you a penny for half of the eggs in your basket."

George shook his head. For the first time in his life he didn't need the money. It was a great feeling. He carried the eggs back to the buckboard while Mrs. Olsten watched in disbelief.

The stranger was wearing a stained overcoat when he reappeared. Some folded newspapers were tucked under an arm. He tossed two bags into the back of the carriage and climbed in.

"The name is Richard Beauchamp Savard," he said by way of introduction. "I'm very grateful for your assistance." He began peeling one of the hard-boiled eggs.

"I'm George Duguay, sir. Your last name sounds French, just like mine. My dad is from Fort William. There's lots of French up there. Mostly fur traders. Where are you from?"

Savard smiled. "I'm from New Orleans," he said between mouthfuls. "There's lots of French folk there too. Have you heard of Louisiana?"

"Yes, sir. Isn't that one of the rebellious states?"

Savard chuckled. "Yes it is. So I guess that makes me a Rebel."

A strange sensation came over George. He was thrilled, yet nervous, to find himself sitting beside a Reb. Men like Savard were fighting against his father.

"There are many Confederate sympathizers in Upper Canada," said George in an attempt to keep the conversation going.

"I'm glad to hear it," said Savard. "Britain and the Confederacy should be friends. Together we can keep the Yankees in their place."

He turned to the young guide and examined him carefully. The boy wore homespun clothes and his shoes were nearly falling apart, but he appeared to be strong and well nourished. In short, he looked and acted like a typical country boy. Well, maybe he seemed a little brighter than most.

"Where is your pa, George?" asked Savard. "Didn't he come into town with you today?"

The response came out so smoothly that it was almost as if it had been rehearsed. "My father has gone away," said George. "I don't know if I will ever see him again."

Although it wasn't exactly a lie, the answer was definitely meant to deceive. The southern gentleman wouldn't volunteer any information if he learned his new friend's father was in the Union army. George knew that Inspector Stansbury would want to hear about the latest Confederate visitor. Although he didn't realize it, George was starting to think like a spy.

The boy obviously didn't want to talk about his father. Savard felt sorry for him. Men sometimes abandoned their families. It was a cruel and cowardly thing to do, but it happened. Savard suspected something like that had happened to the Duguay family. He gave the boy a sympathetic smile.

"This is Mrs. Macdonald's boarding house," said George. He brought the carriage to a halt. "I'll introduce you to her if you like."

"I appreciate the offer," said Savard. "But I can manage." He took some coins from his pocket. "Thanks very much for all your help today."

George had earned another ten cents. It was actually a very generous tip, although it couldn't compare to what the Americans were paying. All in all, it had been an amazingly profitable day. Especially when you considered that he'd also had his hair cut for free by a real barber.

It was time to deliver the letter from the barber shop to the American agents, so George urged Winchester into a trot. The breeze caused some papers to rustle. He glanced under the seat and saw that Savard had forgotten to take his newspapers. They were a welcome find. His mother was always hungry for news of the outside world. She would read every word in both papers.

A short while later he arrived at the Pickford Inn. It didn't particularly surprise him to learn that the Toronto police had also returned. They must still be investigating the attempted killing. Inspector Stansbury and Detective Campbell were chatting quietly on the front porch. Both men caught sight of the boy at the same moment. Stansbury frowned while Campbell gave a friendly wave. The two men had different opinions about most things; and that included what they thought about George.

Five

(Excerpt of letter from Pvt. William Duguay. 11th Michigan Cavalry)

My Darling Wife:

Shortly after I first joined the army I met four brothers from Nova Scotia who'd volunteered together. Yesterday I was talking to the only brother who is still alive. The Rebels got one and disease killed the other two. It must be a terrible blow for their poor mother.

Make sure George keeps the coops in good repair. Chickens won't lay as well if it is drafty . . .

"They paid you all this, just for running a couple of errands?"

Lizzie Duguay was sitting at the family's only table. There were two piles of coins in front of her. A pile of pennies represented payment for all the hard work that had been done by Lizzie, George and hundreds of chickens. The other pile, worth considerably more, was comprised of four small coins made of silver. Sixty cents was more than many men earned for a day of backbreaking labour. Yet her son said he'd earned it by simply delivering some messages.

Lizzie knew that Americans had a reputation for spending money like it was water, but this was ridiculous. Nobody paid that kind of money to a messenger boy. She wouldn't have thought anything of it if George had been paid a few cents. He was always running errands for small tips. The Americans had made a mistake by being overly generous. Lizzie suspected they were up to no good, although she couldn't imagine what.

"You'll have to give it back," she declared. "Every penny."

"Give it back?" George couldn't believe his ears. "But we could really use the money."

"We won't go hungry," his mother said firmly. "Anyway, the army owes your father nearly three months in back wages. He'll send most of it to us when he finally gets paid. Then we'll be fine for a while. I'll be able to keep up our payments to the bank, maybe even buy you some new shoes.

Although George was downcast he knew better than to argue. He recognized the tone of his mother's voice.

As she often did in times of stress, Lizzie glanced at the photograph of her husband on the wall. It was wonderful to have the picture, although she wished he was wearing civilian clothes instead of an army uniform. The uniform reminded her of how much her family had lost to war in the past.

She turned to look at the old musket that hung in a place of honour over the fireplace. The weapon was lovingly cared for, even though it hadn't been fired in years. The oil on the barrel gleamed in the lamplight.

The musket was a veteran of the War of 1812. Lizzie's grandfather, Angus MacDavid, had carried it at the battle of Chrysler's Farm. It was there that a force of British regulars and Canadian volunteers defeated a much larger American army that was attempting to conquer Upper Canada. As the invaders retreated, they took the time to burn MacDavid's farm, destroying everything he owned.

It wasn't the first time the family had paid a stiff price for its loyalty. The MacDavids had once been prosperous landowners in New York State. They sided with the British during the American Revolution. Unfortunately for the MacDavids the British lost the war. Their land was confiscated and they were forced to flee to Canada with all the other Loyalists. They built a new homestead on the north shore of Lake Ontario, only to see it destroyed when war broke out again. Lizzie had been told all her life that the Americans were the enemy. Now her husband was fighting for them. It was enough to make even a strong woman weep.

"I can't say I like this country much." Douglas Chapman spoke in a loud voice, not caring if anyone heard him. He'd been in Upper Canada for less than a week.

Richard Savard shot his countryman an angry glare. "Keep your voice down and mind your tongue," he ordered. "I've told you before; don't do anything to attract attention to yourself." The two men were walking down a busy street and people had turned to stare.

Chapman looked as if he was about to argue, then thought better of it. He was so thin that he appeared frail. In reality Chapman was tough and daring. At age eighteen, he'd been made an officer in a Confederate infantry regiment. He'd been badly wounded, captured, and sent to a prison camp in the northern state of Michigan. From there he'd managed to escape and make his way to Canada.

Quite a few escaped Rebels had started showing up on the Canadian side of the border. The Confederate government quickly became aware of that fact. It even sent a group of special agents to Toronto. Their job was to contact the escaped prisoners and help them get home. Recently the agents had been surprised to discover that someone was getting to the escapees before they did. That person was Richard Savard.

"You have two choices," said Savard. "If you want, I'll put you in touch with a different Confederate organization that will try to get you home. They'll put you on a ship and sneak you through the Yankee blockade. Or you can stay here with me and volunteer for a dangerous mission."

"I wish you'd tell me what this secret assignment was all about," complained Chapman. Savard was firm. "If I told you, it wouldn't be secret, would it? All you need to know right now is that it could be the salvation of your country."

The two men walked silently as Chapman considered his options. He stopped suddenly and pointed towards a construction site. His attention had been caught by a black carpenter. The man was sawing lumber, whistling cheerfully as he laboured.

"I understand there are twenty thousand escaped slaves in Canada," said Chapman. That figure was regularly reported by outraged southern newspapers. Chapman's family owned a large plantation and numerous slaves.

"That's what I've heard," admitted Savard. "There may even be more than that."

Chapman was scandalized. His voice got louder. "Those niggers are worth millions of dollars. They should be returned immediately to their rightful owners. I don't know why you seem to like Canadians so much. They clearly have no respect for other people's property."

Hearing the commotion, the black carpenter looked up from his work. He was startled by the hate he saw in the eyes of the young white man.

Savard grabbed the escaped prisoner's arm and steered him down the street. "It's true the Canadians and British have some peculiar ideas, but we need their help to survive."

"I don't expect these people would be much help in a fight," growled Chapman. "I haven't seen anyone carrying a gun. They all walk around unarmed. Now that's what I call peculiar. It certainly isn't safe."

The American secret agents in Toronto were feeling pleased with themselves. Keeping tabs on the Rebel spy ring was proving to be ridiculously easy. The Confederates spent most of their time in a hotel bar, making grandiose plans and boasting loudly. Everything they said was overheard by interested ears.

What the Americans learned was that the Confederates were content to wait patiently for the so-called Northwest Rebellion to break out. Union casualties had been horrible and many Northerners were calling for an end to the war. There had even been public debates about several Northwestern States leaving the Union and forming a nation of their own. Even though it was mostly just silly talk, the Confederates believed it.

Agents were sent to Upper Canada. Their job was to slip into border states like Minnesota at the first sign of revolution to help organize and train the new armies. However, the rebellions were a surprisingly long time in coming. So the Confederate spies waited and talked and enjoyed an easy life. They had no idea Savard was in town and working on a plan of his own. Neither did the Americans.

Will Bullock and half a dozen other US detectives were sitting around a table at the Pickford Inn. They had the dining room to themselves. Bullock motioned to the maid and she poured him some more coffee.

He waited until Mary Eliza had gone back into the kitchen before speaking. "We'll continue to keep a close eye on the Reb spies. If any of them work up the energy to get off their butts and leave the hotel, it means they're probably planning to slip across the border and cause some mischief. We've got to stop them any way we can."

At that moment, the innkeeper walked into the room with a basket of fresh buns. Alan Pickle put the basket in front of the men, waved off their thanks, walked to the other side of the room and stared absently out a window.

"Do you think the Canadians are aware of what the Rebs are up to?" asked Daniel Benson. He was second in command of the Union spy ring.

"Oh, I'd say so," said a man whose face bore the scars of smallpox. "I'm sure I've spotted at least two of their agents around the Royal Roads."

"Then they've probably got you pegged as well," said Bullock. "Don't forget, they're just as suspicious of us as they are of the Rebs."

Pickle silently left his place by the window and walked to the kitchen. Shortly afterwards, Mary Eliza brought out a fresh pot of coffee, a drink the Americans were much addicted to. She smiled brightly at the men.

"George was wondering if he might have a quick word with you," she said to Bullock.

"The egg boy? Of course I'll see him. Send him in."

George came into the room and sheepishly handed two coins to Bullock. "My mother says I have to give this back to you, sir," he said.

"Why is that?" asked Bullock. "You earned the money fair and square."

"Fifty cents is too much. Ma says honest work doesn't pay that well. She says that anyone who pays that kind of money is up to no good."

Bullock was a smart man and he instantly realized his mistake. If he'd only paid the boy a nickel there wouldn't have been a problem.

"There's no reason you can't keep the money," suggested Benson. "Just don't tell your ma."

The boy would have none of it. "No, sir," he said firmly. "That wouldn't be right."

"All right," said Bullock, reluctantly pocketing the coins. "I hope we're still friends."

"Yes, sir," said George, nodding. "I'll still deliver messages for you if you like, but only as a favour. I can't take any money for it."

As George left the room one of the American agents commented on what a well-raised and remarkably honest lad he was. The others nodded in agreement.

"What about the egg boy?" suggested Colin Campbell. The Canadian detective was walking beside the English inspector on one of Toronto's new wooden sidewalks. The men were discussing ways to keep the American spy ring under observation.

"He visits the Pickford Inn every day. Who knows, maybe he'll overhear something," Campbell continued.

"I'm quite happy with the reports we're getting now," said Stansbury. "They seem to be very accurate."

"True enough," admitted Campbell. "Still, it never hurts to have an extra set of eyes and ears."

"The boy is practically American himself," snapped Stansbury. "His father is in the Union army, don't forget."

The Englishman didn't like Americans very much. They were always slapping you on the back, calling you by your first name, and asking how much money you earned. Even worse, they insisted upon shaking your hand. The practice of shaking hands was still rare in England and Stansbury thought it was disgusting. Just thinking about Americans put him in a bad humour, which wasn't improved by the sight of a familiar figure waiting outside the police station.

"Why there's that tiresome boy now," grumbled Stansbury. "It appears he is waiting for us. Maybe he's going to try and sell us some eggs. If so I'll send him on his way."

Little did he suspect that George had something far more interesting to offer than eggs.

Six

(Excerpt of letter from Pvt. William Duguay. 11th Michigan Cavalry)

Dearest Lizzie:

I can't imagine there has ever been such an army for desertion. The newspapers say there are 100,000 men away from their units. I believe it is true. We lose men every week. Mostly they sneak away at night, put on civilian clothes, and head for home . . .

"I brought you some newspapers," said George, bobbing his head in greeting.

"I don't want to buy a newspaper," growled Stansbury. "And I don't need any blasted eggs either."

George wondered why the Englishman always seemed to be in such a foul temper. "The papers aren't for sale, sir," he said. "I'm giving them to you. A Confederate gentleman forgot them in my buckboard yesterday."

Stansbury was suddenly looking at the boy with a great deal of interest. “A Confederate, eh? What’s his name?” He reached out and snatched the papers. There didn’t seem to be anything unusual about them.

“His name is Richard Savard, sir.”

“Savard? I don’t know that name,” said Campbell, frowning. He thought he knew the name of every Confederate citizen in town.

“Mr. Savard isn’t staying with the other Southerners at the Royal Roads,” said George. “In fact he seems quite determined to avoid the place.”

The two detectives thought about that for a moment.

“Did he say what he does for a living?” asked Stansbury.

“He didn’t say and I didn’t ask,” replied George. “I was afraid to ask too many questions. I didn’t want him to get suspicious.”

Stansbury flipped through the American newspaper for a moment. “Why do you think there’s something in here that might be important?” he asked.

“When I was looking through the papers I noticed that Mr. Savard had circled some of the articles with a pencil. I guessed that those were the stories that interested him the most. I thought you might want to have a look at them,” said George.

“So, which newspaper stories seemed to catch your friend’s interest?” asked Campbell, the big Canadian detective.

“The ones about Britain and the United States possibly going to war,” answered George.

“Do you think you might be seeing Savard again?” asked Stansbury.

George noticed the Englishman’s voice was suddenly sounding a little hoarse. His face was also flushed.

“I hope to see him today,” replied George. “I have to give him his dime back.”

The two detectives then took their young visitor inside to an office and they had quite a long conversation. One of the things they made perfectly clear to the boy was the need for secrecy. His mother wasn't to know a thing.

Richard Savard was perfectly happy with his new boarding house. The room was clean and comfortable and the food was excellent. The Confederate spy had worked late into the night, then slept in, and was now reading a newspaper in the sitting room. It was hard to concentrate on the printed words. His mind kept drifting towards the secret mission. It was almost a relief when his landlady interrupted his thoughts and asked if he'd see a young visitor.

George hadn't told his mother that one of his tips had come from a Confederate that he'd helped. He knew she wouldn't like it. As far as she knew, he'd been running errands for Americans, as if that wasn't bad enough.

Savard had given the egg boy an unusually generous tip because he felt sorry for him. He figured that a family that didn't have a man around could use an extra ten cents. So he was surprised when the youngster insisted that he couldn't keep the money.

"Ma says it's too much," said George for the second time that day.

Savard assumed the mother was too proud to accept anything that smacked of charity. The Confederate knew all about pride. "I understand," he said kindly. He was also impressed that George had given the money to his mother instead of spending it on candy for himself, so he added "You are a good, obedient boy."

George felt a twinge of conscience at being called obedient. Yes, he was obeying his mother's wishes by giving the money back. However, he knew perfectly well that she'd be outraged to learn what he'd been up to in the city.

There were several reasons why George was willing to deceive his mother. Mostly it was because he believed he was performing an important duty for his country. Partly it was because he was growing up and needed to assert some independence. Another reason was that, for the first time in his life, he was having an adventure. It was the most delicious feeling imaginable.

"I can still run errands for you," said George. His expression was friendly and open, as usual. "Or I can take you wherever you want to go in my carriage. If you want you can pay me a penny once in a while. No more than a penny though." He looked and sounded exactly like a humble country boy should.

Richard Savard decided that he liked George very much. He was a naturally warm-hearted man who happened to have a void in his life, having lost his own two sons to scarlet fever. The oldest one had been named after his father. If he'd lived, Richard Jr. would now be about the same age as the young Canadian.

"If you have the time, I'd like to go for a drive down by the docks," said Savard, smiling warmly. "I love looking at ships."

Richard Savard had once been a lawyer in New Orleans, one of the most important cities in the Confederacy. He fled after American forces captured the city. After a harrowing escape by sea he managed to make his way to the British Colony of Bermuda. Now he was living as a refugee in Upper Canada. At least that's the story he told.

George listened wide-eyed, wondering if any of it was true. Even if it was entirely made-up, it was still a great tale. He especially liked the part about Savard being on board a merchant ship that was nearly caught by an American frigate.

"I'm going to return to the South soon and join the army," said Savard. Then he turned solemnly to his young driver. "I hope you support us, George. If the Yankees beat us, they'll come after your country next."

"Do you really think so?" asked George. His concern was genuine. Canadians tended to be deeply suspicious of the United States.

"Absolutely," said Savard. "The Americans have always wanted to annex Canada. To be honest, I don't think there's the slightest chance Britain will be able to hold on to anything west of Lake Superior if the Americans win the war against the South."

George thought about that for a moment. "What if the Confederacy wins?" he asked.

It was exactly the question that Savard had been waiting for. "Then the Yankees are trapped between two great powers," he said. His voice shook with passion. "Britain in the north and the Confederacy in the south. Together we'll be able to make them behave. Britain will even be able to keep her possessions as far west as Vancouver Island."

"What about California?" asked George. He knew the Americans had conquered the rich territory from Mexico just a few years before.

The question disturbed Savard. He had no idea the boy was so well-informed. "I expect California will become an independent nation," he said. "That would probably be best for everyone."

The spy turned and stared into George's eyes, as if trying to read what was in his mind. The eyes were clear and unblinking. Savard was satisfied the boy was guilty of nothing except youthful curiosity.

George knew he'd made a mistake. Detective Campbell had told him to be friendly and helpful, but not to seem too intelligent. It would be best if Savard underestimated him. Time to change the subject.

"Americans sure can be a nuisance," sighed George. "My own family has had to fight them twice."

He knew at once that he had Savard's attention. So George told the story of how his mother's family had remained loyal to the King during the American Revolution and lost everything they owned. Then came the War of 1812, when the family's new homestead was destroyed by the invaders.

"My great-grandfather fought at Chrysler's Farm," said George proudly. "His younger brother was killed at Queenston Heights."

"I don't recall learning about those battles at school," commented Savard. "I'm sure that if they'd been American victories I'd have heard of them," he added wryly.

The spy allowed himself to daydream for a moment. He thought of disciplined British troops marching south from Montreal, of Canadian militia launching fierce raids into New York State, and of the Royal Navy smashing the Union blockade. With allies like those, the Confederate army was certain to win. It wasn't just a dream either. Savard knew in his heart that it could happen. *If* he did his job properly.

A new thought suddenly struck him and he turned to George. "By the way," said Savard. "Did I leave some newspapers under your seat when you helped me move the other day?"

"Nope. I haven't seen them," said George casually. The lie came out as smooth as silk.

Seven

(Excerpt of letter from Pvt. William Duguay. 11th Michigan Cavalry)

Dearest Lizzie:

I saw my first big fight yesterday and it wasn't pretty. Our infantry attacked the Rebel positions and were cut to pieces. Then the Rebs charged our lines, yelling at the top of their lungs. I'm ashamed to say our infantry ran away. Our artillery did a good job though. If the enemy had artillery as good as ours they'd have won the war by now.

I've now been given most of my back pay, which I'm sending to you . . .

Toronto's waterfront was bustling with activity. The docks were filled with sailors on leave, merchants looking for bargains, and stevedores soaked with sweat. An American steamer was pulling into a wharf, her flag fluttering brightly in a light breeze. Richard Savard's eyes narrowed when he spotted the ship.

George carefully steered Winchester around parked wagons and piles of boxes. The calm old gelding plodded on, ignoring all the noise and activity. Savard didn't pay any more attention to the hustle and bustle than the horse did. He only had eyes for the ships. The newly arrived steamer was particularly interesting to him.

The scouting trip was working out exactly as the Confederate had hoped. Nobody paid the slightest attention to a man and boy riding in a battered old buggy. They could easily have been father and son. Savard couldn't have asked for a better disguise.

Once they'd driven past all the docks and warehouses, Savard asked to turn around and make the tour again. George gladly obliged. Pleased with what he'd seen, Savard began to whistle a lively tune.

"What song is that?" asked George after listening for a while.

"Catchy isn't it?" said Savard. "The song is called 'Dixie'. It's so popular in the South that it's almost our national anthem."

"I've never heard of it," said George.

Unexpectedly, and to the boy's delight, Savard began singing loudly. "I wish I was in the land of cotton. Old times there are not forgotten. Look away, look away, look away, Dixie land."

"Stop it! How dare you sing that song here!"

A young man was walking towards them, his face distorted by hatred. He held up his left arm to show that the hand was missing. "I joined the great crusade to end slavery," he said hoarsely. "It cost me my hand."

The man walked up to the buckboard and stood close to Savard, attempting to stare him down. "If you're smart, stranger, you'll drive away and watch your tongue from now on."

Unafraid, Savard stepped down from the buckboard and faced his accuser. The men stood almost nose-to-nose.

"I understand that Dixie is even popular in the American army," said Savard in a low voice. "It seems like a lot of people like the song. I guess I can sing it here, seeing as this is a free country."

"That's right," snapped the one-handed man. "This is a free country. We have no human bondage and no use for the songs that slave-keepers sing."

Both men were angry. More insults were exchanged. In a fury, the newcomer pulled out a knife with his good hand. Savard barely managed to jump out of the way of the slashing blade.

George saw everything from the buckboard. He realized the young man was very fast and extremely dangerous. Savard also knew he was in trouble. He cursed the fact he was following the local custom and didn't have a gun.

Suddenly an egg smashed into the attacker's forehead. Bright orange yolk flew into his eyes and temporarily blinded him. He reached up with the stump of his missing hand and began to wipe away the thick liquid. The point of his knife waved uncertainly. The Confederate was a man who thought on his feet. Not wasting a second he stepped forward and punched his assailant in the stomach. The man let out a loud grunt and dropped to the ground.

Savard turned and jumped into the waiting buggy. "I think we'd best be going now," he said urgently. The advice was unnecessary. George was already whipping Winchester into a trot.

Savard glanced back, smiled at the sight of a crowd gathering around the fallen man, and started singing again. "In Dixie land I'll take my stand. To live and die in Dixie!"

Then he let out a triumphant whoop that sounded more animal than human. A shiver went up George's spine. He knew he'd just heard the famous Rebel yell that had terrified so many

Union soldiers. Flushed with excitement he tried his own version of the yell.

Savard roared with delight and slapped the boy on the back. “You saved my skin by tossing that egg, George. I guess that makes you an honorary Reb. Let me hear you try that yell again.”

Grinning, the boy tilted back his head and yelped as loud as he could.

“That’s pretty good. Now listen to how a real Rebel does it.”

Savard’s piercing howl terrified poor Winchester into a full gallop. It had been years since the old nag ran that fast.

Captain Jacob Thompson paced impatiently outside the boarding house, working himself into a fury. The landlady, a trusting soul, had obligingly confirmed that Richard Savard was one of her guests.

Thompson was supposed to be in charge of all Confederate intelligence activities in Canada. It had come as an unwelcome surprise to learn that Savard was in Toronto. The two men disliked each other intensely. One of Thompson’s government friends had tipped him off that Savard was working on his own secret project.

Thompson had sent one of his agents to deliver a lengthy letter to Savard, ordering him to report at once to Confederate headquarters at the Royal Roads Hotel. Two days later, there still hadn’t been a reply, so Thompson decided to take matters into his own hand.

"People have found fault with my singing before, but that man was the nastiest critic yet," Savard chuckled. He spoke loudly, so as to be heard above the rattling of the buckboard.

"I was afraid he was going to gut you like a fish," said George. He'd now witnessed two attempted murders, in addition to being nearly shot himself. It was enough to make you shake your head in wonder. "Why did that man hate 'Dixie' so much? I think it's a pretty tune."

"That song is a symbol of my nation," said Savard. "That misguided fool obviously hates the Confederacy." A thought occurred to him and he looked under the seat. He could have sworn he'd left those newspapers there. No sign of them though.

"It sounded as though he joined the Union army to fight against slavery." George knew what Savard was looking for. He wanted to get the man's mind on something else, even if it meant saying something inflammatory.

"Slavery!" snapped Savard. He instantly forgot about the papers. "This war has nothing to do with slavery."

George was genuinely surprised. "If it isn't about slavery, than what is it about?"

"It is about people having the right to decide their own government." Savard fought to keep his voice under control. He was becoming extremely fond of George and he didn't want to appear as if he was lecturing the boy.

"Think of the United States as a club. States like Louisiana and Virginia willingly joined, didn't like the ways things were going, and decided to quit. Only now the Yankees say we can't leave. That's nonsense of course. If we had the right to reject British rule in 1776, how come we can't legally leave the United States today? I tell you, George, those Yankees have a double standard."

It was a speech Savard had made many times before and he passionately believed every word. "I assure you that Abraham Lincoln is a worse tyrant than King George the Third ever was. And that's really saying something. As we all know, old George was totally insane."

George's feelings appeared to have been hurt. "I was named after King George," he said quietly.

Savard immediately apologized. He'd forgotten the boy came from Loyalist stock. George nodded his forgiveness. In truth, he wasn't insulted at all. He'd only been having a little fun with the Confederate. George was named after an uncle, not the mad king who'd cost England half a continent.

Inspector Stansbury and Detective Campbell worked surprisingly well together, considering they couldn't stand each other and disagreed on almost everything. They even had to overcome their very different opinions on the American civil war.

Stansbury liked most of the Confederates he'd met. They seemed to be more British than American in the way they talked and acted. It was unfortunate that the South believed in slavery, but the inspector was convinced that would change. He predicted that if the Confederacy won its independence slavery would gradually be abolished over the next twenty or thirty years.

A Confederate victory, in Stansbury's opinion, would also ensure that the Americans didn't annex Canada. However, he'd reluctantly concluded the southern states were destined to lose. The North simply had too much money and too many men.

Campbell, on the other hand, got along very well with Americans. He thought they were friendly and generous. The detective was also a passionate abolitionist who wanted an end to slavery. Although Campbell fervently hoped for a Northern victory he'd almost given up hope. The Rebels seemed to be much better fighters. They had embarrassed one Union general after another. Also, an increasing number of Americans were calling for peace.

Where Stansbury and Campbell did agree was on the need to keep Britain out of the conflict. The previous year, when war with the US seemed likely, the British had sent army reinforcements to Canada. Ten thousand troops were all that could be spared. The number was pitifully small. American generals seemed to think nothing of losing ten thousand men in a single battle.

Great Britain had a huge navy, but a small army. Even worse, those soldiers were spread around the world, policing the largest empire the world had ever seen. There was no way enough men could be shipped to Canada in time to fight off an American invasion.

Campbell and Stansbury agreed that England must remain neutral. So they buried their differences and worked together, keeping a wary eye on Confederate and Union agents alike. They were prepared to use every tool at their disposal, and that included George the egg boy. They were already referring to him as the youngest spy.

"Do you own any slaves?" asked George. He hoped the question didn't offend Savard, yet he was terribly curious to learn the answer.

"Nope," was the response. "Most people in the South don't have coloured servants of their own, which is more proof the war isn't about slavery."

Savard shifted his weight on the hard wooden seat. They were just a couple of blocks from his boarding house and he was looking forward to getting out and having a stretch.

"Do you know any nig . . . ah, Negroes?" asked Savard.

"No," admitted George. "But there are some in Toronto. One family lives in a house not too far from here. I go by it all the time."

Savard knew Canadians had a reputation of being soft on blacks, so he tried to be gentle. "They are a simple folk. No more than children, really."

"I hear the Americans are recruiting coloured troops now," said George.

"That just goes to prove how desperate the Yanks are," said Savard. He was unable to keep the sneer from his face. "Coloured troops are no match for our boys."

He was about to say more on the subject, but they'd arrived at the boarding house. Standing by the side of the road was a sour-faced figure that Savard recognized immediately. It was the insufferable Jacob Thompson. The man who was in charge of the official Confederate spy network in Toronto. The man Savard had hoped to avoid.

"Hello, Jacob. Haven't seen you in years." Savard kept his voice level as he swung down from the buckboard.

"Don't 'hello' me," snapped Thompson. "You have a lot of explaining to do."

Savard gave a contemptuous shrug and turned to George. "Here's two cents for your trouble. I hope I'm not paying you too much this time." He gave the boy a warm smile.

"Don't turn your back on me," warned Thompson. His face was contorted with rage.

"You'd best be going now, George," said Savard quietly. He gave Winchester a sharp slap on the rump. The horse grudgingly interrupted his break and began to walk forward.

The boy nodded his thanks and put the pennies into his pocket. He watched from the moving carriage as the two men walked towards the boarding house. Savard led, ignoring the man who was following half a step behind.

"Didn't you get my letter?" bleated Thompson. He followed Savard through the front door.

"I sure did," said Savard over his shoulder. "I read it and then I put it in the outhouse where it belongs." The door slammed shut.

At that exact moment George pulled on the reins with all his strength, bringing his startled horse to an immediate halt.

Eight

(Excerpt of letter from Pvt. William Duguay. 11th Michigan Cavalry)

> *My Darling Wife:*
>
> *I regret to say that I've been very sick. I spent the last two days in a hospital. It was so terrible that I refused to stay there any longer. The doctors are all fools or drunks and they kill more men than they save. I'd rather take my chances in camp with the rest of the men. I'd appreciate it if you could send me medicine for my stomach. There is none to be found here . . .*

George was only able to find the last two pages of the letter that Savard had brought to the outhouse. They'd been left on top of a pile of torn newspaper, destined to be used as toilet paper.

Inspector Stansbury read the rescued pages for the third time. "The first page is missing," he said unhappily. He handed the documents over to Detective Campbell, who had been waiting impatiently for his turn to read them.

"I wasn't going to climb down and get it," said George defensively.

Stansbury couldn't blame him. Nobody would voluntarily go into the pit of an outdoor toilet, especially now that the weather had turned hot.

"Did you read the letter?" asked the inspector. He looked at the boy suspiciously.

"Sure. I didn't want to bring you something that wasn't important."

The letter was certainly important. It proved that the Confederates in Toronto were split into two camps. Richard Savard had arrived by himself and was now setting up his own organization. The man who was supposed to be in charge of all Confederates spies in Toronto didn't appreciate the competition. Jacob Thompson was ordering Savard to disband his men, end his "reckless adventure" and leave Canada immediately.

"This certainly complicates things," said Campbell after he'd finished reading.

Stansbury nodded his agreement. It was important to find out more about the reckless adventure that Thompson had written about.

"I don't want you to say anything about this to your American friends at the Pickford Inn," he said to George.

Asking the boy to provide information on the Confederates was one thing. His father was fighting them after all. Stansbury never pressured George to spy on the Americans. That would be asking too much. Besides, he already knew everything that was said and done at the Pickford Inn.

The inspector opened a desk drawer and took out a battered cash box. From the box he removed five one-dollar bills and offered them to George.

The boy took a step backwards and firmly shook his head. "There is no way I'm climbing down into that outhouse and getting that piece of paper for you. Not even for five whole dollars."

"I'm not asking you to do that," said Stansbury. "This is for services already rendered."

George clearly didn't understand.

"The information you brought us is very useful," continued Stansbury. "This is your reward."

Once again George was astonished at how well-paying the spy business could be. However, there was no way he could accept the windfall. His mother would only make him take it back.

Stansbury closely examined the youngster standing before him. He noted the rough clothes and shoes that were falling to pieces. "Take the money. I'm sure your family can use it."

"I can't take your money" said George firmly. He turned and ran from the room.

The inspector's jaw dropped as he watched George flee. "What on earth was that about?"

"Perhaps he was insulted by your offer of money," commented Campbell. He rarely missed a chance to toss verbal darts at the Englishman. "Maybe he's a true patriot who wants nothing more than the chance to help his Queen and country."

"Oh, I doubt that," scoffed Stansbury. "Don't forget that his father is a common mercenary. He joined the American army just for the money."

"Poor people often have some tough choices to make," said Campbell. His voice was soft. "George's father chose to risk his life so his family could have a farm of its own. Every army is full of men who fight for the money. I think you British call it 'taking the Queen's shilling'. To their credit the Americans pay considerably more than that."

Stansbury was deeply offended. "What do you mean by *you British*? You're British too."

Campbell smiled. "Well, it's not quite as simple as that. It used to be that only the French in Quebec called themselves Canadiens. Things are starting to change."

Captain Jacob Thompson was nursing a splitting headache. The Confederate spymaster blamed his discomfort directly on his arch-rival Savard. The meeting between the two men at the boarding house had not gone well. They'd argued violently over Savard's refusal to explain his mission or to call it off.

Sitting alone in a comfortable hotel room, rubbing his aching forehead, Thompson had come to an unpleasant conclusion. Although it was sooner than he'd planned it was time to start the Northwest Rebellion. He had to do something dramatic before Savard won all the glory.

"You've been drinking on the job again, Poulin."

Constable Paul Poulin of the Toronto police force denied the accusation. It was pointless. The smell of his breath gave him away.

Detective Campbell's smile did not make Poulin feel any better. If anything, the grin seemed quite sinister. "I've got a job that will soon sober you up."

"What's that?" asked Poulin. His lower lip trembled. He suspected he was in danger of losing his job.

"You'll be fetching a letter for me."

That didn't seem too bad. Poulin began feeling a lot better about his immediate future.

"C'mon Rebs, time for breakfast. You get half-rations today. Yep, instead of two beans you get just one."

Sergeant Perry Mott roared with laughter, although no one else joined in. A long line of ragged men shuffled forward. Each one carried a battered tin plate and a spoon. A few faces turned and stared at the American prison guard with open hatred. Mott loved tormenting the Confederates prisoners at every opportunity. The prisoners were being punished because two of them had managed to escape. The prison camp's already skimpy rations were being cut in half. They'd remain that way for a week, or until the escapees were caught, whichever came first.

There were nearly three thousand Confederate captives on Johnson's Island Prison. It wasn't a pleasant place, but at least it was better than most Civil War prisoner-of-war camps. Instead of ragged tents, the men actually had wooden barracks to live in. Although the buildings were crude, they provided some shelter from the rain and the winds that constantly blew off of Lake Erie.

A stockade made from thick planks surrounded the camp. Armed guards stood watch from the blockhouses, ready to shoot at any Reb who dared to try and escape. At least that was the theory. In reality the guards were just as bored as the prisoners. They spent their time napping, playing cards or reading. A few, led by the brutal Sergeant Mott, amused themselves by bullying the prisoners.

The Southerners wore the same clothes they were wearing when first captured. Ragged bits of brown and grey uniforms hung from skinny bodies. At least half the men had no shoes. The food was terrible. Mostly the men had to make do with rice and beans. Sometimes there was a little salt fish or picked beef.

The prison guards, brutish as they were, weren't the biggest killers of men . That dubious honour belonged to disease. Epidemics regularly swept the camp and killed scores of prisoners.

At first, few Confederates attempted to escape. The North and the South conducted regular prisoner exchanges. The value of a prisoner depended on his rank. A private was traded even-up for another private. A general was worth forty-six privates. If a prisoner was patient he would almost certainly go home again. All he had to do was swear an oath that he wouldn't take any further part in the war.

However, the prisoner exchanges had recently stopped. It was all because the Americans had started using black soldiers. The Confederacy announced that any Negro soldiers it captured would either be executed or sold as slaves. The Union response was to call off all prisoner exchanges. Now that there was no longer a chance of going home quickly, the Confederate prisoners on Johnson's Island began to despair. The first prison break had taken place during the winter. A handful of men managed to get out of the stockade and walk across the frozen lake to Canada.

It wasn't long before almost every prisoner was working on his own escape plans. Getting past the stockade was the hardest part. You had to tunnel under it or climb over it. Those who went over the top risked getting shot by the guards.

The island was in a harbour, a short distance from the town of Sandusky, Ohio. A strong swimmer could make it to the mainland with little trouble. Weaker men could lash primitive rafts together from driftwood. The two who had just escaped were more creative. They had managed to sneak on board a small steamship that had stopped at the island to deliver supplies.

If they managed to get off the island, escapees had two choices. They could try to reach their homes by crossing hundreds of miles of hostile American territory, or they could turn north and head for nearby Canada.

A young man in clergyman's clothes knocked loudly on the boardinghouse door. There was no answer. Everyone was out. This was going to be easier than expected. The minister was actually a Toronto police officer in disguise. If someone was home he was to pretend he was lost and ask for directions. Luckily the landlady had gone to the market. The disguised policeman turned from the door and made a discreet hand signal.

"That's the all-clear signal," said Detective Campbell. "Go and get it."

Constable Poulin, who was now sober and wearing civilian work clothes, trotted reluctantly towards the outhouse at the back of the building. He was already looking as if he was going to be sick.

"I'm glad he's not wearing his best suit," chuckled Campbell.

Billy Bacon thought he couldn't possibly run any further. His heart was pounding so hard that it felt as if it was about to burst through his ribs. A bullet kicked up a spray of gravel near his heels. Sheer terror flooded through him and gave him the energy to keep the legs moving.

"For God's sake, Billy, try and keep up." Alexander Beauchine looked over his shoulder. Some American soldiers had been tracking the two escaped prisoners for several hours. Now they were now within musket shot.

The Confederates ran through a thicket. Bacon tripped and skidded along the ground. It turned out to be a lucky thing. The bullet that would have hit him in the back passed harmlessly overhead, snapping a sapling in half.

"We're done for," groaned Bacon. With a superhuman effort he pulled himself up and lurched forward.

"That's the river up ahead," gasped Beauchine. "Don't give up yet."

The day had gone so well for Monroe Huntoon that he felt like he'd died and gone to Heaven. In any event, he knew he'd never see a prettier angel. Monroe had been madly in love with Angie Frances his whole life. It was entirely one-sided. Angie never showed the slightest interest in him. Every time Monroe had asked if she'd like to go for a walk or a boat ride, she'd turned him down. He'd recently asked her to go on a picnic, and to his unexpected delight, she'd agreed. It was only because all the interesting young men were off at the war, but he didn't know that.

Monroe's mother made a fabulous lunch for them, delighted that her awkward but persistent son was finally making some progress. There was a popular picnic spot in some secluded woods along the Detroit River that could only be reached by boat. At first Angie was reluctant to get into the small craft. Monroe finally coaxed her into the boat and began to row. After a while she started to relax. At one point she even smiled, which nearly caused her overjoyed companion to burst into tears.

When they arrived at the picnic spot Monroe jumped out of the boat. He grabbed the rope that was tied to the bow and looked for a suitable tree to tie it to.

"Who are they?" asked Angie. She pointed towards two filthy men running towards them.

Almost as soon as Monroe looked up, he was pushed roughly to one side and the rope was yanked from his hand. The two strangers jumped into the boat.

"I insist that you get out right now." scolded Angie. She had little patience for bad manners.

"Sorry, miss," said Billy Bacon. He tipped his ragged hat politely. Then, without another word, he grabbed Angie's legs and tipped her from the boat into the river.

"How dare you!" roared Monroe. An oar crashed down on his head and he collapsed onto a rotten log.

Alexander Beauchine was a strong rower who knew how to handle a boat. They quickly pulled away from the shore. A few moments later, a group of blue-coated soldiers spilled out of the bush. Their attention was immediately drawn to the young woman who screamed that she was drowning. It took several seconds before they realized that all she had to do was stand up and wade to shore. That extra time made all the difference to Bacon and Beauchine. It allowed them to get a little further out into the river.

"These Michigan boys aren't exactly sharpshooter material," commented Beauchine dryly. Small splashes clearly showed where the bullets were hitting the water. So far nothing had come close.

"If they were Kentucky men we'd be dead by now," agreed Bacon. He opened the basket he'd found in the stern. "Well isn't this nice. They've even packed lunch for us."

"And we've almost made the Canadian side." Beauchine was breathing hard as he strained on the oars. "Yes, this is our lucky day."

Nine

(Excerpt of letter from Pvt. William Duguay. 11th Michigan Cavalry)

Dear Lizzie:

It appears I'm an ignorant fool who doesn't even know why this war is being fought. Some of the men in my troop laughed when I made a comment about the war being fought to put an end to human bondage. They insisted the struggle is about preserving the United States, not about freeing slaves. Cpl. Higgins went so far as to say he volunteered to fight for Uncle Sam, not for Uncle Sambo.

My stomach is feeling much better. I'm glad George is able to do most of the farm work himself. I can't imagine any father has ever had a more reliable and honest son . . .

A piece of paper can sometimes determine the fate of nations. Even if it's a just a filthy letter fished out of an outhouse by a retching police officer. Constable Paul Poulin, much against his will, had earned a place in history. He'd done it by retrieving the first page of the note that Richard Savard had rudely sent to the outhouse. The document proved Savard was attempting to cause a war between the United States and Great Britain. Unfortunately, the letter didn't actually say what the plan was.

"It's time to kick all the Confederates out of Canada," complained Detective Campbell. "They've finally given us the excuse we need."

"Can't do it." Inspector Stansbury shook his head firmly. "At least not yet. The Confederates will just claim that Savard was acting on his own. It could even be true. This letter clearly warns him to stop whatever he's doing."

Stansbury stared at the piece of paper lying on the desk in front of him. "Who cleaned it off?"

"Constable Poulin. We found him drunk on duty this morning. Getting the paper and cleaning it off was his punishment."

"Oh. How's he feeling?"

"I understand he's resigned from the force."

The inspector nodded sympathetically. "I can't say I blame him."

Constable Poulin had had enough of being a peeler. There was too much dirty work involved. He ran off and joined the American army, which didn't mind if a man had a drink now and then.

Poulin was pleased with the size of the bounty he was paid for signing up. In fact he was so impressed that he decided to make a career of it. He deserted from his unit, went to a different town, rejoined the army, collected another bounty, and deserted again. Poulin successfully did this nearly a dozen times before he was caught. He was a fairly wealthy young man by the time the Americans hanged him.

Billy Bacon and Alexander Beauchine agreed again that they were the luckiest men on the face of the earth. It was an amazing fluke that they'd stumbled upon the rowboat just as they were about to be cornered by the Yankee soldiers. Then they'd rowed through a hailstorm of bullets without a scratch. Now they were free men in Canada. Even better, they were free men with full stomachs. The picnic lunch they'd found in the boat was delicious.

They walked along a dusty country road enjoying the sense of freedom. They spotted a well-built farmhouse ahead.

"Do you think we should stop and introduce ourselves?" asked Bacon.

Beauchine nodded confidently. "I figure that Montreal is just a few miles away," he said, displaying an appalling lack of geography. "We just have to get pointed in the right direction."

"Do you think it's safe to go up to the house?" Bacon was the more cautious of the two.

"Sure. Canadians don't like the Yanks any more than we do. They'll be glad to see us. I'll bet they insist we stay for supper."

Bacon nodded his agreement. The two men walked up to the farmhouse and knocked on the door. Then, just to make sure the homeowner knew he had some special guests, they let out a chorus of Rebel yells.

"Who's there?" demanded a startled voice from inside the house.

"We're Confederate soldiers," shouted Bacon. "We escaped from a prison camp in the US If it isn't too much to ask, we'd like some water and maybe a ride to Montreal."

"Confederates?" The voice was disbelieving.

"That's right."

"Well hold on then. I'm coming."

The two escaped prisoners were still grinning at each other when the door swept open and they found themselves staring at the business end of a musket. The man holding the weapon didn't look like he had much love for the Confederate cause. He was black. Billy Bacon and Alexander Beauchine had just run out of luck.

"I can't believe it, he actually came back here." Mary Eliza shook her head in disbelief. She was helping George carry baskets of eggs into the kitchen.

"Who?" said George.

"Alonzo Wolverton. He's the man who paid you the Confederate dollar and then nearly got shot." Mary leaned closer land her voice dropped to a whisper. "He's a natural-born traitor, you know."

"What do you mean." George glanced around to see if anyone else was listening. It was the first time anyone had told him what the man's name was or why someone had tried to kill him.

Keeping her voice low, Mary Eliza explained that Wolverton was a refugee from the war. It was suspected that he was also a deserter, although no one was certain which army he'd belonged to. Perhaps he'd belonged to each of them for short periods of time. After arriving in Toronto he began doing jobs for the Confederate spy ring. Then he offered his services to the Americans as well.

"The Confederates must have figured out what was going on," said Mary. "I'm sure that's why somebody tried to kill the scoundrel."

"Why did he come back?"

"He needs some cash," sniffed Mary. "He's always asking for money. Mr. Bullock gave him a few dollars and sent him away."

Mrs. Pickle walked into the kitchen. She wondered why the two young people stopped talking the moment they saw her. Could there be romance in the air? It didn't seem likely. Mary Eliza was too old for George.

Meanwhile, Pickle had also been thinking about Alonzo Wolverton. He knew he should report the man's visit to Inspector Stansbury, but he didn't want to. Pickle was a reluctant informer. He was only passing on information because he was afraid of what Stansbury might do to him. The British detective had told him that unless he spied on the Americans, the Pickford Inn would mysteriously burn to the ground. So, out of fear, the innkeeper passed on every bit of information he picked up from his guests.

Pickle hated spying on his countrymen. He decided it was time to rebel. The late-night arrival of Alonzo Wolverton was the first bit of information that would not be passed on to the arrogant Englishman.

Richard Savard needed tough men to make his plan work, but that didn't mean he was willing to accept everyone who knew how to use a gun. Frank Happa was a dangerous and unpredictable character. He probably would have ended up as an outlaw or common murderer if the war hadn't come along. Although born in a northern state, Happa elected to fight for the Confederacy. He joined a notorious band of guerillas that burned and murdered its way through Union towns. After being seriously wounded, Happa was captured and sent to a prison camp. He'd recently joined the ranks of escaped prisoners who'd managed to make their way to Canada. Now he was being interviewed by Savard.

"I hear you tried to kill a man the other day," Savard said dryly. He'd finally learned about the attempt on Alonzo Wolverton's life. What he didn't know was that Happa had also wanted to eliminate George as a witness. He'd never have forgiven him for that.

Happa shrugged and smiled, displaying a row of chipped and stained teeth. "My aim ain't what it used to be. My arm got shot up and I'm learnin' to use t'other hand." He rubbed the stiff shoulder. "I'm still clumsy."

"Who ordered you to shoot Wolverton?"

The smile turned to a sneer. "Nobody. I decided to take care of the traitor myself." That was a lie. He'd been working for Jacob Thompson.

"Well you didn't do a very good job of it. Wolverton got clean away. Even worse, the shooting got the local authorities all riled up."

Happa shrugged again. He'd never cared very much what anybody thought of him. "I'll do better next time."

Savard's voice cut like a whip. "There won't be a next time! Not if you join me. I won't have my plans ruined by a hothead who goes off and shoots at people just for the sport of it."

He desperately needed men who weren't afraid of a fight. Happa certainly fit the bill, but he lacked discipline. Savard thought about his options.

"Well, what about it?" Happa was tired of waiting for an answer. "Am I in?"

"Hand over your gun."

Happa looked at Savard in disbelief. "My gun? Are you crazy? Nobody takes my gun from me."

"Then you don't get to join us," said Savard firmly.

Happa knew he didn't have a lot of choice. The Canadians were looking for him, the Americans would probably shoot on sight, and the official Confederate spy ring no longer wanted anything to do with him. He was friendless and penniless in a foreign land.

"I'll need a little cash to see me through," said Happa, reluctantly handing over his pistol. "I've been sleeping under bridges and I haven't had much to eat for a couple of days."

Savard handed over a few bills. "Let me know as soon as you find yourself a room. And try to keep out of trouble."

Things weren't going well for Billy Bacon and Alexander Beauchine, the escaped Confederates. The black farmer had tied them tightly together and driven them in a wagon to town. The farmer spat in both their faces, gave each of them a vicious poke with the barrel of his musket, and then handed them over to the mayor. Not knowing what else to do, the bewildered mayor locked the two men in his root cellar and sent for the army.

That's when Bacon and Beauchine had another amazing turn of good luck. The man who came to see them was a Canadian army officer with strong southern sympathies. In fact, Colonel George Taylor Denison was actively working for the Confederacy. He told the two runaways that he was going to send them to a hotel in Sarnia, where more than fifty escaped Confederates were staying. From there they would eventually take the train to Toronto to meet with a very special agent.

Two big Union victories, nearly on the same day! Savard read the newspaper with disbelief. The Yankees had finally defeated the main Confederate army at a place called Gettysburg. Even worse, the great Confederate fortress of Vicksburg had fallen after a long siege. Now the entire Mississippi River was in American hands. The South was cut in two.

Now, more than ever, the Confederacy desperately needed a powerful ally like Great Britain. The sound of carriage wheels outside brought Savard to his feet. He ran downstairs, knowing who had just arrived.

"You're running behind today, George."

"Yes, Mr. Savard. Sorry about that." George wondered why the Confederate looked so grim. He hadn't yet heard about the two Union victories.

Savard gave the horse an absentminded pat on the muzzle while the boy climbed down from the wagon. "I imagine you know most of the farmers around here."

George nodded as he picked up a basket of eggs. He'd been born and raised in the area.

"Do you know any who support the Southern cause?" asked Savard.

"Albert Trawick does," George said instantly. "His son is a doctor in the Confederate army."

"Do you know Trawick?"

The boy laughed out loud. Trawick was one of the biggest landowners in the area, one who had a personal connection to the Duguay family. "He used to be our landlord," said George.

Savard prompted the boy to tell him everything he knew about Trawick and the size of his property. He seemed very satisfied with what he'd heard. "Do you know how to get to Trawick's estate?" he asked.

"I sure do. It isn't far from our homestead. There's still a lot of forest out there, so sometimes I go hunting near his land."

"Hunting?" There was a thoughtful look on Savard's face.

"Mostly just rabbits at this time of year. My mother lets me go sometimes on Sundays after church."

"You know, George, roast rabbit is one of my favourite foods. I don't imagine that you'd be willing to take me hunting, would you?"

It wasn't rabbits the Confederate wanted to bag; George was certain of that.

Ten

(Excerpt of letter from Pvt. William Duguay. 11th Michigan Cavalry)

Darling Lizzie:

I have seen my first coloured troops. They marched in good order and looked sharp, but nobody knows for sure how steady they'll be in a fight. I guess we'll find out soon enough. The American army has taken so many casualties that it needs every soldier it can get, no matter what colour their skin. The Confederates hate the Negro soldiers with a passion. They murder every black prisoner who falls into their hands . . .

George spoke firmly. "I have some news for you, but you have to promise not to pay me anything."

Inspector Stansbury rolled his eyes. "All right, I promise," he said dryly. "Not so much as half a penny, no matter how good the information is." He could see Detective Campbell in the background, nearly bursting with suppressed laughter.

"I don't know if this is important or not," continued George. He was relieved that no one was going to try and tempt him with cash. "Mr. Savard asked me if I knew any farmers with Southern sympathies. Didn't want to know about any town folk. He was only interested in farmers. I told him about Mr. Trawick."

"Who is Trawick?"

Campbell immediately jumped in. "He's one of the richest men in the area. Trawick has a huge chunk of land just outside the city. His son is serving with the Rebels as a physician. I believe the young man was practicing medicine in Atlanta before the war broke out. He'd married a southern lady while attending college."

George explained how Savard wanted to know everything about Trawick's farm. "Then he asked me to take him hunting on Sunday. I'm pretty sure he wants to have a look at the area for himself."

"What did you say?" asked the inspector eagerly. "Did you agree to go with him."

"I said I'd ask Ma."

Stansbury leaned forward and gripped the boy's shoulder. "You must go hunting with Savard," he said firmly. "I don't care what you tell your mother. Run away from home for the day if you must. Just make certain that you are there to help him slaughter bunnies."

"It would certainly be a big help to us," Campbell added gently.

George looked slowly from one man to the other. He certainly didn't mind the idea of going hunting with Savard. On the other hand, he hated making a promise to the policemen that he couldn't keep. There was no guarantee his mother would give him the day off. Often there were chores that needed to be done and he'd recently promised to repair one of the chicken coops.

"All right," George said, a little reluctantly. "I'll do it." He turned to go, then changed his mind. "I almost forgot to tell you, Alonzo Wolverton is back in town. He's the saddle tramp who nearly got killed, remember? Anyway, he showed up at the Pickford Inn last night. The Americans gave him some money and sent him away."

Then he casually walked out of the room, unaware of how much trouble he'd just caused for a certain innkeeper.

George's life had always been quiet and predictable. He did his chores, went to school when there was time, and never complained when times were tough. Like every other youngster he dreamed of adventure, but never really expected to have one.

Now, although almost everyone thought of him as a country bumpkin, he was doing important work for his country. Being a spy was often confusing, and sometimes it was even frightening, but George was eager for more. He was having the time of his life.

Humming happily, the song happened to be Dixie, George drove his buckboard towards home. On impulse he turned down the street where the Negro family lived. They had a neat house surrounded by a picket fence. Two young children played a noisy game of tag in the yard. A couple of chickens scratched in the grass. Even city residents often kept a few chickens for their own use. Curious, George brought the wagon to a halt and stared at the children. He'd never been so close to black people before.

"Hello there." It took a moment for George to realize someone was calling to him. Startled, he noticed a woman walking from the house. She'd evidently seen him through the window.

"You're the egg boy aren't you?" The woman was tall and lean and very dark. She wore a red bandana over her hair. "Mrs. MacIssac says you deliver to her."

Embarrassed at being caught gawking, George was on the verge of giving Winchester a lash of the reins. Then the woman smiled, which showed she wasn't annoyed.

"You haven't come by here before," she said, walking up to the buckboard. The two children stopped playing and watched curiously.

George's newfound expertise in lying came in handy. "No ma'am. I knew you had chickens of your own and weren't likely to need eggs from me. I was just, ah, looking at your hens to see what kind they are."

The woman glanced at her hens and nodded approvingly. "Javas, mostly. We get lots of eggs from them."

"Sorry to bother you," said George politely. "I guess I should be going now."

"Not so fast," said the woman, holding up a hand. "I have all the eggs I need, but I don't have any spare birds to slaughter. Would you be able to sell me a couple of fat chickens? I'm having a special supper on Monday. A very special supper."

To George's astonishment her eyes filled with tears, which she quickly brushed away.

"I can bring you a couple of roasters," said George. He was embarrassed for the woman. "They'll be fat and tender. You can count on it."

It had turned into a very bad day for Alan Pickle, the owner of the Pickford Inn. Someone had told Inspector Stansbury about Alonzo Wolverton's late night visit to the inn. The Englishman had demanded to know why Pickle hadn't told him about the saddle tramp's arrival. Unsatisfied with the lame excuses that he heard, the policeman threatened to throw the innkeeper into jail. He made it clear there had better be no more treachery.

Pickle wondered who had told on him. It had to be one of the American agents staying at the hotel. Several of them had been present when Wolverton was given some money and told to scram. One of them must be feeding information to the British. Pickle was reluctant to confide his suspicions to Will Bullock, the head of the American spy ring. What if word got back to the traitor? Pickle's life might be in danger. The wise thing to do was keep his mouth shut and his eyes open. Maybe he'd be able to figure out who the informant was.

"Would you like some more tea, Mr. Pickle?" Mary Eliza walked into the office where he was working. She smiled at him. "You look as if there's something troubling you, sir."

Pickle started feeling better. Mary Eliza had a knack for making everything seem a little brighter than it really was. "Thank you for your concern, Mary. Everything is fine. And yes, some tea would be very nice."

Like most Americans Pickle preferred coffee to tea, but Mary Eliza had never learned how to make a decent pot of coffee. It was safer to go with tea.

After the maid had gone, Pickle took a letter out of his vest pocket and methodically tore it to pieces. The letter had been enough to ruin his day. It was from his sister in New York City. Her youngest son, a spoiled boy of eighteen, had just been drafted into the army. He was afraid of being killed, so the family had decided to send him to stay with his uncle in Canada.

"Here I am with an inn full of American agents," he moaned quietly to himself. "They won't be impressed to learn I'm giving shelter to a cowardly nephew."

"Is it okay if I go hunting on Sunday?"

Lizzie Duguay looked up from her sewing. She was sympathetic to her son's request. He was doing a man's work and rarely had any time for himself. It would probably do George some good to get out into the forest for a few hours. Besides, some fresh rabbit would be a welcome change from chicken.

"I suppose you can go," said Lizzie. "I'm just a little concerned about when the floor of that chicken coop will finally get fixed."

"I'll fix it. I promise."

"Okay then. We'll go to the early church service and then you can go."

George smiled. Things were working out just fine.

"You go tomorrow," said Jacob Thompson, the official Confederate spymaster in Toronto. He stabbed the air with his cigar for effect. Two of his best agents listened expectantly.

"In a couple of days you'll meet up with our agents in Illinois. They have guns, money and men. Now's the time to organize a secret army in the American Northwest. There are at least four states where people are tired of the war. We think they'll soon choose to leave the United States, just like we did. Your job is to help them organize."

The days of plotting and waiting were finally over! The agents were excited at the prospect of actually going into action. They knew that if the secret plan worked, the survival of the Confederacy was guaranteed.

Thompson was putting his plan into action sooner than he'd originally planned. The Confederate spymaster knew that Richard Savard would soon be launching his own operation. Thompson was determined to beat his rival to the punch. He wanted to make sure that he, not Savard, went down in history as the man who saved the Confederate States of America.

Eleven

(Excerpt of letter from Pvt. William Duguay. 11th Michigan Cavalry)

My Darling Wife:

My troop was out on patrol yesterday and we ran into some Confederate soldiers. Instead of shooting at us, they waved us over and said they wanted to do some trading. They had whiskey and tobacco, which they traded for all the spare food we were carrying. The rebels are a very ragged bunch. Most of them don't have proper uniforms. Some don't even have shoes. They seemed to be half-starved.

I was glad to get the note from George. His handwriting is getting much better. I hope he hasn't gone back to using his left hand . . .

George had no idea it was possible for a girl to run so fast in long skirts. Mary Eliza hurtled down the stairs of the Pickford Inn's front porch at breakneck speed. Even Winchester neighed in surprise at the sight of her.

The maid reached the buckboard. There was a wild gleam to her eyes. "Things are starting to happen," she gasped. She stopped for a moment beside the buckboard and drew a couple of deep breaths.

George stared in amazement. Mary Eliza took a quick glance over her shoulder to make sure no one was watching. Then she leaned close to George and whispered urgently.

"You must get a message to Inspector Stansbury right away. Tell him that two Confederate agents are heading for the main train station. They're being tailed by two Union agents. The Americans are named Martin and Cruz. They've been told to make certain the Rebels don't cross the border alive. The Americans have infiltrated the Confederate spy ring and they've uncovered a hare-brained plan to start another rebellion."

"How do you know all that?" asked George. His face actually betrayed some surprise, which pleased Mary Eliza immensely.

"Never mind. It's enough that I know you're working for us as well, so stop gawking and do what I say."

Mary Eliza reached up and took two baskets of eggs from the buggy. "I'll make sure you get paid for these later. Now get going!" She turned and gave Winchester a hard slap on his rump. The startled horse jumped forward.

Mary Eliza composed herself as she watched George's buckboard race away. She knew it was important to look and act normally when she went back inside the inn. Mary, the pretty little maid who was always flirting with the guests, was becoming a very competent intelligence agent.

The two Confederates didn't want to look as if they were travelling together. They arrived at the train station separately and didn't even look at each other while they waited. One of them boarded the train and found a seat in the front carriage. The second man pretended to read the newspaper for a while. Then he casually climbed into the second car and took a vacant seat.

If he'd been a little more careful he might have noticed the two figures that slipped out from behind a pile of luggage and got into the last carriage. Martin and Cruz, the two American agents, had been told not to allow the Confederates to cross into the US under any circumstances.

The conductor waited impatiently for a large immigrant family to get its luggage sorted out. When the last bag was aboard, he waved to the engineer. The engineer waved back and blew the train's whistle. Steam poured from the stack as the locomotive started to move forward.

To the conductor's extreme annoyance, three men appeared out of nowhere. They ran along the passenger platform and pulled themselves onto the moving train. Detective Colin Campbell and two other Canadian agents had arrived in the nick of time.

The conductor confronted the new arrivals. "It's dangerous to jump onto a moving train," he lectured. "You fools are lucky you didn't break your necks. Show me your tickets."

"We're the police," said Campbell, breathing hard. "We don't need tickets." He pushed past the startled conductor and went in search of his prey.

The two American agents had made themselves comfortable in a small private compartment. A deck of cards was being shuffled. The men had some time to kill before taking care of the Confederates.

"We're on the Grand Trunk Railway," said Martin as he dealt the cards. He was always looking for an opportunity to show off his knowledge. "It's the longest railroad in the world."

"Is that a fact?" responded Cruz. He couldn't believe his good fortune. He'd been dealt three aces. "The longest in the world, huh? I never would have thought the Canadians could pull off something like that."

Just then the door opened and a large man stepped inside.

"Sorry pal, but this is a private compartment," said Martin. "We aren't looking for any company."

But the unwelcome stranger didn't apologize and back out the door. Instead he opened up his jacket to show he was carrying a pistol in a holster.

"Permit me to introduce myself." The man's voice was unusually soft, considering how big he was. "I'm Detective Colin Campbell. Queen Victoria has asked me to keep on eye on you two." He noticed that Martin's hand was edging towards a coat pocket.

"Don't do it, not unless you're a lot faster than I think you are. Besides, two of my men are in the hallway. They're both armed as well."

"What do you want from us?" croaked Cruz. He gave Martin a kick under the table. It was a warning not to try anything funny.

Campbell noticed the gesture and smiled his approval. "We know you followed a couple of Confederate agents onto this train. Having a naturally suspicious mind, I think you mean to do them harm."

The Canadian detective sat down on the bench opposite Martin. "I want you boys to understand that I am no lover of the Southern cause. It wouldn't bother me at all if you slit the throats of the men you're following and dropped them off a bridge. I just don't want you to do it on Canadian soil." Then he raised his voice for the first time. "Don't do anything horrid, like commit murder, until you are back in the US. Am I making myself clear?"

The two American agents nodded unhappily. They were already wondering what their boss would say when he discovered the mission had failed.

Campbell stood up and opened the compartment window. For a moment he simply stood there, as if enjoying the fresh air and the passing scenery. Then he turned to Martin. "Take off your coat and give it to me. Keep your hands away from the pockets."

Martin reluctantly handed over his coat. To his fury Campbell threw the garment out the window. "What did you do that for?"

"Because there was a gun in the pocket. You aren't supposed to be carrying one in this country. You know the rules." Campbell gave the American a hard look. "You look like the sort who keeps a knife in their boot. Hand it over."

With a contemptuous flick of the wrist, Martin tossed the knife from his boot right out the window.

"Nicely done," said Campbell. He was genuinely impressed with Martin's knife-throwing talent. "Now toss the boots out too."

"Make me," growled Martin. He'd finally had enough.

"All right, I will," said Campbell cheerfully. "I'm warning you though. Those boots will still be attached to your feet when they go through the window."

Martin considered his options for a moment. Then he sighed, took off his boots, and watched as they sailed out of view.

Campbell turned to Cruz. "What about you?"

Cruz handed over a matched set of pistols. "They are a present from my wife," he said. "I would consider it a favour if you didn't throw them away."

The Canadian looked at the pistols with open admiration. They were the latest models and very expensive. "You're right. They are much too nice to toss from a train. I think I'll keep them myself."

Then he pretended to notice the cards on the table for the first time. "It looks like you boys were set to have a game of poker. I've heard that you Americans are fond of the game. Never played myself, but I'd like to learn. What do you say, boys? It's going to be a long train trip. Why don't you pass the time by teaching me how to play? I've got a few dollars if you'd like to play for money."

In truth, Detective Campbell already knew how to play poker. He was actually so good that no one in the Toronto police department would play with him any more. The Americans scowled. Neither one was in the mood to play cards.

Campbell ignored the glares. He shuffled the deck and began dealing. "So," he said conversationally, "are you enjoying your visit to Canada?"

Archie Chittendon's first impressions of Canada certainly weren't favourable. There was so much construction in Toronto that the city had a half-built appearance. It certainly wasn't as grand as his hometown of New York City. His uncle's inn wasn't nearly as comfortable as he'd thought it was going to be either. The room he'd been assigned was hardly larger than a closet.

The young man had recently received a letter from the American government that ordered him to report for army duty. It was something he had no intention of ever doing. The law allowed you to hire a replacement, but that would cost around three hundred dollars. Although Archie's parents were prosperous they were also thrifty. They thought it would be cheaper, and safer, if they sent the boy to live out of the country for a while. Surely the war couldn't go on for much longer.

A letter had been sent to Uncle Alan in Canada, informing him that Archie would soon be on his way. However, with mail service between the two countries being extremely unreliable, the letter arrived in Toronto just a few hours before Archie did.

Pickle's surprise reunion with his nephew took place in front of half a dozen American spies. The boy, not knowing who his uncle's guests were, expressed relief at successfully avoiding the draft. His countrymen, who were already fighting a secret war, were not impressed. They expressed their feelings of disgust so strongly that a terrified Archie locked himself into his tiny room and refused to come out.

"I still say you are being very pig-headed about this." Inspector Stansbury's fingers drummed a military beat on the desktop.

"I'm sorry, sir. I know it doesn't make any sense to you." George eyed the door, planning his escape.

"Why on earth won't you let me help you?"

"I'm sorry. It's hard to explain."

The inspector reached out his hand, causing the boy to recoil. "What you are doing isn't natural, George. You've been providing us with very useful information. You have done your country and your Queen a great service. For God's sake, take the money!"

George stole a glance at the bills clenched in the Englishman's hand, then firmly shook his head. Queen Victoria's secret service operated around the world. It had countless agents, informers and traitors on the payroll. George Duguay was the only one who refused to accept a single penny for his work. Perhaps he was the only spy in the world who still worried about what his mother thought.

Twelve

(Excerpt of letter from Sgt. William Duguay. 11th Michigan Cavalry)

Dearest Lizzie:

I've been promoted to sergeant. I'm not sure why. I guess it's because they think the other men will do what I say. The old sergeant deserted. He'll hang if they catch him. The promotion means I'll get paid more. I must admit that there is decent money to be made in war . . .

The rattlesnake was stretched out on the road, basking in the morning sun. At the sight of the serpent Winchester put on the brakes and refused to take another step.

"I didn't realize you had rattlers in Canada," commented Savard. "He's got an interesting pattern on his skin."

"That's a Massassagua rattler," declared George. "I know a boy who got bit by one a couple of summers ago. He almost died."

Savard looked at the snake with interest. "So how do you propose we get rid of that varmint, George? Should we shoot it or whack it with a stick?"

"I'll show you what Ma taught me." George climbed carefully down from the buckboard. He knew the snake could feel vibrations in the ground. Heavy footsteps would spook it, causing it to coil up and prepare to defend itself.

The boy walked as quietly as he could towards the serpent's tail. Savard sat speechless, entranced by what he was witnessing. When he was within an arm's-length of the snake, George pounced. He grabbed the tail and, with a single fluid motion, snapped the snake as if it were a whip. Then he casually tossed the limp body into the ditch.

"That breaks their spine," he explained as he climbed back into the buggy.

"Your ma taught you how to do that?" Savard shook his head in disbelief.

"They have lots of rattlers around Niagara, where she grew up. She says the girls used to have contests to see who could kill the most snakes in a day."

Savard roared with laughter. "Now I understand why Canadian men don't need to carry guns; they've got their womenfolk to protect them."

"How did things go?"

"Good," said Detective Campbell. "Once we reached the border we gave the Confederates a ten minute head start. Then we let the Union boys go after them. Of course, Martin the American won't be moving very fast until he gets a new pair of boots."

"Why does Martin need new boots?" asked Inspector Stansbury.

"Because he carelessly dropped them out of the window of a moving train. He's a slow learner. He lost his coat the same way." Campbell took a pair of pistols out of a small bag. "What do you think of these?"

Stansbury looked at the weapons with interest. "Colts. Very nice. Where did you get them?"

"I took them from Cruz. He said they were a present from his wife. That will make me cherish them even more."

Stansbury couldn't help but smile. Although he had his differences with the Canadian detective he occasionally enjoyed the man's odd sense of humour. "How did you pass the time on the train?"

"We played poker."

"Oh dear." Stansbury knew all about Campbell's reputation with cards. "Did you leave them with any money?"

"Not even enough to buy their next meal." Campbell grinned contentedly.

"That's the road to the Trawick farm," said George. He brought the buckboard to a halt. Large trees lined the route.

"It looks as if a lot of the estate is still heavily forested," commented Savard. He nodded his head approvingly. "I wonder if Mr. Trawick would be willing to let a Southern visitor and his young friend hunt on his land? I think we should ask him."

A private road snaked through the woods, skirted a very large pasture, and finally ended at a grand old house. Two large barns and numerous outbuildings stood near the house. Everything was a little untidy, as if things weren't being kept up the way they used to be.

As the buckboard rattled to a halt, the front door to the house opened and a stooped figure stepped out. Albert Trawick was bald and wrinkled. To George he looked ancient. He didn't seem happy to see the visitors either.

"Who are you?" he asked gruffly. He'd briefly met George once, several years ago, and clearly didn't remember him.

Savard jumped nimbly down from the buggy, took off his hat, and bowed elegantly. "Please forgive me for dropping in unannounced," he said politely. "I was passing by your farm when my young friend," he gestured towards George, "mentioned your name and said your son was serving the Confederacy as a doctor."

Savard took another step forward. His hands began to tremble and it looked like he was trying to keep from crying. It was a masterful acting job and George admired it tremendously.

"I was once in the Confederate army myself," continued Savard. "I was badly wounded in battle and only the skill of a young surgeon saved my life. After I'd recovered I went to thank the doctor. He told me his name was Trawick and that he was from Canada." Savard's voice was nearly breaking with emotion. "Please forgive me, sir, but when I discovered that you lived here I simply had to stop in and thank you for raising such a fine son."

Trawick's expression had completely changed. His face was now split by a huge, toothless smile. "You know my boy?" he croaked happily. "Please come in and visit for a while."

"I'd hate to impose upon your hospitality," Savard said smoothly. "Besides, I promised George I'd take him rabbit hunting. He's itching to go."

"The boy is more than welcome to hunt on my land," said Trawick. He pointed an unsteady finger to the north. "See that thicket over there? There's a rabbit under every log. They're always raiding my garden. It would be nice to see them thinned out."

Savard appeared to consider the idea for a moment. "Well, you honour me with your invitation." He turned to George. "Would you mind hunting by yourself for a while?"

The boy's expression never changed, but there was a twinkle in his eyes. "I don't mind at all."

"That settles it then," said Trawick, chuckling. He shuffled towards the door. "I'll tell the maid to get out some of her baking."

"That was quite the performance," said George admiringly. He watched the old man go inside. "Did you have it memorized or did you make it up on the spot?"

"I guess it was a little of both." Savard beamed at his young friend. He was genuinely fond of George. "Don't give me away, okay? I'll do you a big favour in return some day. I hope you aren't upset I won't be hunting with you."

"That's okay. I didn't really expect you to anyway, seeing as how you didn't even bring a gun along."

Savard gave him a friendly slap on the back and walked towards the house.

George put Winchester into a small pasture that had both clover and fresh water. Then he grabbed his father's musket from the back of the wagon and walked towards the bush.

"Let me get this straight. You want us to cross back into the United States, get captured, and let ourselves be sent back to Johnson's Island Prison." Billy Bacon shook his head in disbelief.

"That's exactly what I'm asking you to do. I know it sounds odd."

"It's not odd, it's downright crazy," snarled Alexander Beauchine.

Lieutenant John Headley just smiled and nodded calmly. He understood perfectly well why the two men didn't want to go back to prison. After all, he was an escaped Confederate prisoner of war himself. Recently he'd been recruited to take part in a daring adventure. Now he was looking for other volunteers.

"I darn near starved to death at Johnson's Island," complained Bacon. "Why on earth would I want to go back there?"

Bacon and Beauchine were staying at a hotel in Sarnia with about fifty other escaped Confederate prisoners. They didn't know who was paying the bills and they didn't particularly care. The important thing was that they had comfortable beds, all the food they could eat, and nobody expected them to do any work.

The men had originally been told they would all be smuggled back home. Now they were being asked if they'd be willing to volunteer for a very important mission instead.

"Why should it be us?" Beauchine glared at the Lieutenant. "There's lots of other escaped prisoners. Why don't you ask some of them?"

"Because you are the most recent escapees," Headley explained patiently. "It wouldn't look as suspicious if you were the ones recaptured."

"We're not gonna do it," Bacon said defiantly.

"There would be quite a bit of money in it for you."

"Doesn't matter, we're still not gonna do it," snapped Bacon. There was a short pause. "How much money?"

Alexander Beauchine didn't like the direction the conversation was turning, so he jumped in. "Money doesn't do much good for a man who can't spend it because he's in prison."

"The money would be waiting for you when you got out. We'd put it in a nice, safe Canadian bank." Headley looked from one man to the other. "The best part about it is that you wouldn't be in prison for very long. We'll get you out again."

"How do you propose to do that?" Billy Bacon was becoming intrigued with the idea in spite of himself.

"I can't give you any details until you've signed up," said Headley. "But I can tell you that what we are about to do will astonish the entire world."

Thirteen

(Excerpt of letter from Sgt. William Duguay, 11th Michigan Cavalry)

My Darling Wife:

I've been thinking a lot about George lately. There are many boys in both armies and some are even younger than he is. Last night I helped hold down a wounded drummer boy while the surgeons cut off one of his arms. I pray that my son never has to pick up a musket in defence of his Queen and Country. I worry that England and the United States will go to war. George and I could find ourselves wearing different uniforms. I'd refuse to fight against my own country, of course, for which the Yankees would hang me . . .

The hunting was every bit as good as Mr. Trawick had promised it would be. The woods of his estate were thick with rabbits and partridge. George even saw plenty of sign of deer and bears. He wandered contentedly through the bush, committing paths and landmarks to memory. After he'd bagged half a dozen rabbits George wandered back to the manor house.

Mr. Trawick congratulated the successful hunter and happily accepted half of the kill for his own supper. It turned out that Savard had completely won the old man's trust. He'd even been invited to spend the night.

"Good shooting, George," said the Confederate. "Mr. Trawick tells me that his cook makes a superb rabbit pie. I can hardly wait to taste it."

"You're welcome to stay for supper as well, lad," said Trawick.

"Thanks for the invitation, sir. My ma will be expecting me home shortly, though."

George suspected that neither man really wanted him around. It appeared there were things they wanted to talk about. So he accepted one of the sticky buns that Trawick offered and politely said goodbye. Savard volunteered to come outside and help harness Winchester.

"You did me a big favour by bringing me here, George. I won't forget it."

"That's okay. I had a good day myself."

Savard looked like a man with a lot on his mind. "I guess you don't live too far from here," he said absently.

"About three miles away," said George. "You just keep to the right every time you come to a junction in a road. Then, when you cross a small bridge over a creek, you see our farm."

The creek was the same one that passed through Trawick's property. Paths ran along its banks and George was certain you could follow them all the way from his farm to Trawick's. He was just about to mention that when Savard interrupted him.

"I hope you didn't have any trouble getting your ma to give you the day off."

"Nope," said George. "As long as I repair that chicken coop tomorrow afternoon."

"What needs to be done to it?"

"Oh, nothing much. There are a few rotten boards on the floor that have to be replaced. I'll do it when I get home from delivering the eggs. My mother probably won't even be there. She'll be visiting with some of her friends. They're making a quilt."

Savard thought about it for a moment. "You know, George, I'd be pleased to lend a hand. I'm a pretty fair carpenter, if I don't say so myself."

George was so startled he couldn't immediately think of a response. Luckily, Savard was buckling up a piece of harness and didn't notice the boy's discomfort. The last thing George needed was for his friend to show up at the farm. His mother had no idea that Savard even existed. She would be furious to learn that her son was spending time in the company of a Confederate. Undoubtedly she would make a point of telling Savard that her own husband was fighting for the Union side. Then she would order him off her property. It would be a disaster. Savard would realize that there was a lot more to George than he'd suspected.

George felt his knees trembling, so he took a deep breath and tried to stay calm. Then he said the words that are almost always used at the beginning of the biggest lies.

"I have to be perfectly honest with you." George stared at the ground, hoping it made him appear to be embarrassed. "I've never told my mother about you. She's the strongest abolitionist you can imagine. She hates the Southern cause. If she knew I'd made friends with a Confederate she'd be furious."

When George looked up to see what impression his lie had made he was astonished to see tears in Savard's eyes. The Confederate took a step forward and hugged the boy.

"Thank you for being so honest," he said, sniffling a little. "And thank you for extending the hand of friendship to me, despite what your ma thinks. George, if I am ever blessed with another son I hope he is exactly like you."

A few minutes later, fervently thanking God for his narrow escape, George was in the buckboard and pulling away from the farm.

Mr. Trawick had come onto the porch to wave goodbye. "You can come back to go hunting any time you want," he called. "Don't even bother to come and ask permission. Just go ahead and do it."

It was an invitation that George had every intention of accepting.

"She's a beauty." The grizzled old sailor was being completely sincere. He'd been on a lot of ships over the past fifty years and had an expert eye. "She's got some of the most graceful lines I've ever seen on a steamer."

"Thanks, old timer." The first mate beamed in pride. "I think she's the finest steamship on the Great Lakes."

The Island Queen was tied to a dock on the Toronto waterfront. Her passengers were long departed and burly stevedores struggled to unload cargo from the American ship.

"Allow me to introduce myself," said the stranger. He'd been standing on the docks, admiring the ship since she'd come in to dock. "I'm Captain James Bates."

"I'm assuming from your accent that you're not Canadian," commented the first mate.

"Nope, I'm American just like you. My daughter married a Canadian seaman. I'm retired now, so I live with them here in Toronto."

"Would you like to have a look around?"

Bates was delighted by the offer. "That would be the kindest thing you could do for an old sea-dog like me," he said. "I'd love to see the Island Queen up close."

So the friendly sailor took Captain Bates on a lengthy tour of the ship and patiently answered all of his questions. The young man had no idea that he was dealing with a famous Mississippi riverboat captain with a violent grudge against the United States. His beloved river was under the control of Union gunboats and his own ship had been captured and burned.

Bates had recently arrived in Toronto, met the man who'd recruited him, and got his orders. He was certainly looking forward to carrying those orders out.

"We'll have to fight the British and Canadians eventually, so we may as well get it over with." Daniel Benson was cleaning his fingernails with a knife. The Union detective spoke with a little too much emotion, resulting in a nasty cut.

"Calm down, Dan. As President Lincoln says, one war at a time." One of the reasons Will Bullock had been put in charge of the American spy system in Toronto was because he kept a cool head. "The British burned Washington during the War of 1812. We don't want to give them an excuse to try and do it again."

The two men had just received a message saying that the mission to kill the two Confederates on the train had been foiled. Benson felt the British and Canadians were being unreasonable. Why should they care if a couple of Rebel spies suddenly disappeared?

"The British sell ships and supplies to the Confederates," complained Benson. "They are no friends of ours."

"It's not that simple," explained Bullock. "The British upper classes support the Confederacy, that's true. I guess there isn't much difference between an English duke and a Southern plantation owner. But the important thing is that most ordinary Englishmen hate slavery. That goes for the Canadians too. The longer the war goes on, the more support we'll get from them."

Benson snorted. It was obvious he wasn't convinced.

Bullock decided to change the topic. "So, is Pickle's cowardly nephew still in his room?"

An evil smile flickered across the other man's face. "I guess he doesn't have much choice, seeing as how we've nailed the door shut."

"You'll just have to be patient, Archie. I've got two of the nails out, but there are still three to go." Mary Eliza leisurely worked away with the claw end of a hammer, prying at a nail. The maid saw no need to rush. Like everyone else at the inn she didn't think very highly of the young guest from New York City.

"Can't you go a little faster?" asked a plaintive voice from the other side of the door. "I'm starting to feel very uncomfortable, if you know what I mean."

"I'm going as fast as I can," said Mary Eliza. She stopped to gaze at her own reflection in a hallway mirror.

There was a short silence, followed by, "Mary, why is everyone being so mean to me?"

The maid rolled her eyes in disbelief. Pickle's nephew was remarkably dense, even for a man. "Because virtually everyone staying at the inn is a strong Union supporter. In fact, most of your uncle's guests are agents of the US government. They don't think highly of someone who ran away so he wouldn't have to fight in the war."

Mary Eliza waited for a reply, but all she heard from behind the closed door was a series of thumps and crashes. It sounded as if somebody was tearing the tiny room apart. She stifled a giggle and waited expectantly.

"Mary?" There was real pain in Archie's voice now. "Are you still there?"

"Still here."

"There doesn't seem to be a chamber pot in this room."

"Oh dear, that is a problem," said Mary Eliza. "I wish I could say you'd be free soon. Unfortunately I'm not very good with tools. I'm having a terrible time getting these nails out." In fact, she was hardly trying at all.

"Then what am I to do? I feel as if I'm about to explode. Please excuse my bluntness. I don't know what will happen if I don't get immediate relief."

"How about using one of your boots?" suggested Mary Eliza. It was a struggle to keep from laughing too loudly.

"A boot? Surely you're joking." Archie was outraged.

"You can always empty it later," she replied.

Mary Eliza examined the nail she'd been trying to pull out of the door. She was reluctant to damage it. Nails were quite expensive. Nevertheless, her desire to punish the cowardly Archie exceeded her natural thrift. Mary Eliza gave the nail a sharp whack with her hammer.

"What rotten luck!" she cried. "I accidentally bent a nail. This is going to take even longer than I'd thought."

Fourteen

(Excerpt of letter from Sgt. William Duguay, 11th Michigan Cavalry)

Darling Lizzie:

I was talking to a Confederate prisoner and discovered he was from New Brunswick. He sailed to New Orleans in '58, married a local woman, and joined the Rebel army in '61. He claims to hate slavery and says he spoke out against it so strongly that some of the men in his company threatened to bullwhip him. Even so, he is loyal to the Southern cause and is convinced the rebellion will succeed. What a peculiar war.

Thank you for writing regularly. Your letters bring me great comfort . . .

The same two Negro children were playing in the yard when George pulled up in his buckboard. They smiled at him shyly. One of them shouted out to his mother that the egg boy had arrived.

Their mother poked her head through the kitchen window. "Are those my roasting hens?" she called out, smiling. "I hope they're fat, 'cause I'm going to have a house full of hungry people tonight."

George picked up two squawking birds by their feet and walked to the house. Whenever possible housewives preferred to buy their meat while it was still alive. That was the only way they could ensure that it was fresh. George waited on the step until he heard, "Don't be shy, boy. C'mon in."

While the lady of the house focused her attention on the chickens, poking them with expert fingers, George glanced curiously around. He was mildly surprised to learn that these people seemed to live the same way his family did. There was nothing remotely foreign or exotic about the surroundings. The furniture was rough, but the house was spotless. Curiously, a Union Jack was tacked to the wall above a rocking chair.

Two men sat at the kitchen table. One appeared to be about sixteen. He wore spectacles and seemed quiet and studious. The other man was old enough to have a few grey hairs. Even though he was sitting down, it was obvious that he was unusually tall. They interrupted their conversation to nod pleasantly at the newcomer.

George heard the woman say, "These are fine birds."

"Thank you, Mrs. . . ?

"Cobb. Don't bother with formalities though. Just call me Bessie, like everyone else does." She took some money out of a worn purse and handed it to George.

He nodded his thanks. "Are you having a special dinner tonight?" he asked. Now that the chickens had been accepted he was waiting to see if the woman wanted him to slaughter them.

Bessie was trying to be cheerful, although her smile was strained. "Special is right. For one thing, it could be the last decent meal they get for a while." She gestured towards the two men.

The men noted her fragile frame of mind and exchanged glances. Then the older one spoke. "I wish you'd join the army with us, Bessie. At least then we could count on good grub." He had a booming, pleasant voice that any preacher would envy.

The comment took George by surprise. "Which army?"

"The American army, for sure," said the man, smiling hugely. "The Confederates sure as blazes don't want us." He laughed heartily at his own joke.

"Bob is our special guest," explained Bessie. "He's been staying with us ever since the Underground Railway delivered him to Canada last year." Then, just in case George hadn't figured it out yet, she added, "He's a runaway slave."

Bob's smile faded. "It ain't just a white man's fight any more. The Union needs coloured troops if it's gonna win the war, so I'm off to be a soldier."

"I'm going too," said the young man softly. It was the first time he'd spoken since George's arrival. "It isn't fair to expect white boys to take all the risks."

"This is my son Charles," said Bessie. There was both sadness and pride in her voice. "He's also going to join the crusade against human bondage."

"Have you been following the progress of the war?" asked Charles. He sounded more like a gentle Sunday school teacher than a soldier.

"My mother and I follow it very closely," said George. "My father is fighting with the American army."

To his astonishment Bessie burst into tears. She seemed embarrassed by her display of emotion.

"I'm sorry," she sniffled. "It's just that war is so horrible. Men are killed and maimed. Women lose their husbands and sons. Children are left without fathers." A sob wracked her body. "I promised myself not to cry today."

"There ain't no need to feel shame," Bob said kindly. "Tears jus' prove you have a soul."

Charles looked at his mother with concern, but couldn't think of the right thing to say. He squirmed silently in his chair.

Bessie wiped away her tears and turned to George. "It must be hard on your poor ma, to have your pa so far away."

"It bothers her more than she lets on," he replied. "Between the American Revolution and the War of 1812, her family lost pretty much everything. Now she worries about what might happen in this war."

The black woman blinked in surprise and pleasure. "Your ma from Loyalist stock?"

The boy nodded.

"So are we," Bessie said proudly.

George was flabbergasted. He had no idea there could possibly be such a thing as a coloured Loyalist. "Where is your family originally from?" he asked.

"Maryland. During the Revolution the British offered to free any slave who was willing to fight for them. It was a better deal than what George Washington offered. That man was a slave-owner, don't forget. My great-grandpa joined with the Redcoats. After the war, the British gave land grants to the coloured Loyalists, mostly in Nova Scotia." She nodded towards the Union Jack hanging from the wall. "That flag has been in the family since the Revolution."

"It's the flag 'o freedom, boy, and that's the truth." Bob's voice rumbled through the room. He got up from his chair, towering over everyone else. Then he bent over so he could look George in the eye. "When I was yer age I lived on a cotton plantation. I was no better than the pigs or the cows. One of the ole slaves had a picture of a British ship. I can't imagine where he got it. Every time he showed it to me he'd point at the flag and say, 'There's the flag of freedom, Bob. You go where that flag is flyin' and you won't ever have to call anyone Massa agin. That's why I runned away and came to Canada. Now I'm a free man."

A short while later, George left the house, having been treated as an honoured guest. There was a lot on his mind. He wondered if Bob and Charles were eligible for generous signing bonuses, like the Americans gave to white soldiers. Somehow he doubted it.

Richard Savard was very satisfied with how his plan was unfolding. Old man Trawick had volunteered the use of his isolated estate. Bates, the Mississippi steamboat captain, had the heart of a pirate and was thirsting for revenge. The veteran sailor agreed that the Island Queen was perfect for the job ahead.

In an amazingly short time, Savard had managed to create a private army. The escaped Confederate soldiers had left Sarnia in small groups and were gathering at a secret camp. Before he led those desperate men on their hazardous mission, there was one more thing Savard planned to do. He wanted to say goodbye to the boy.

A Highland regiment marched through downtown Toronto, cheered by the crowd. Bagpipes skirled and kilts rippled in a strong breeze. Most of the Jocks, as the soldiers were called, were recruited from the industrial slums of their homeland. The underfed offspring of the working poor, they often had a stunted appearance. When the Highlanders arrived in Canada they were astonished to discover that even the local women sometimes towered over them. To them it appeared as if this big, new land was growing oversized people.

Detective Colin Campbell was smoking a pipe outside the police station when George arrived to make his report. They stood together and watched the soldiers march by.

"Do you like the sound of bagpipes, or are you a music lover?" asked Campbell. He laughed at his own joke.

"It's an odd sound," replied George. "I understand it makes the Highlanders fight even harder." The soldiers reminded him of Bantam roosters, small but tough.

"They don't need much of an excuse to fight," said the detective. He knocked ash out of his pipe. "Did you know the British won't allow two Highland regiments to camp beside each other? They say nothing good can come of it. Either the regiments will fight each other or they'll join forces and start a rebellion."

They watched the kilted figures march past. "Have they been sent here to protect us from the Americans?" asked George.

"Yes. Every time the Yankees do a little saber-rattling, England has to put the Royal Navy on alert and send more troops to Canada. The British government is getting very tired of dancing to the same old tune, which is good news for us."

"What's so good about that?" asked George, astounded by what he'd heard. Like most Canadians he took comfort in British military might.

Campbell put some more tobacco in his pipe and tamped it down with a thumb. "It's no secret that England wants us to take on more responsibility for defending ourselves. That means we're going to have to raise a permanent army instead of relying on the Redcoats. Colonies don't have armies. Nations do."

The detective lit his pipe with a flaming match. He sucked on it reflectively for a moment before continuing. "Mark my words; we're going to get a country of our own very soon. There's talk about all the British colonies in North America joining together. They'd better. If they remain separate, the US will swallow them up one by one. "

Campbell's eyes were bright as he watched the last of the Highlanders disappear around a corner. "You know, it's almost funny. The Americans had to fight for their independence. We're going to get ours handed to us on a silver platter. I wonder if we'll appreciate something that comes so easily."

George's head was beginning to hurt. Politics was unbelievably complicated. "I guess we'd better go inside so I can give my report to the inspector," he said.

"So what is Savard up to?" asked the detective. He opened up the door.

"Well, he certainly seems to have won the trust of Mr. Trawick," said George as he walked inside.

On the other side of the street a rough-looking man stepped out from the cover of a doorway. He stared at the police station, thinking hard. Frank Happa, the renegade gunslinger, had been drinking in a bar when he'd heard the sound of the bagpipes. Curious, he went outside to watch the Highlanders parade past. While there he'd caught sight of a boy who looked oddly familiar. The youngster was talking to a man who was obviously a policeman. Eventually Happa remembered where he'd seen the boy before. He angrily spat onto the street and stalked away.

A short while later Happa was at Savard's boarding house, only to be told by the landlady that she had no idea where her guest was. Happa accepted the kind woman's offer of a cup of coffee. He was sipping it in the living room when there was a knock at the door. His hostess said it was just the egg boy, then she scurried off to see what he wanted.

Happa heard a youthful voice asking about Savard. Curious, he peeked through the doorway and recognized George. Fate had delivered the troublesome boy to him.

Fifteen

(Excerpt of letter from Sgt. William Duguay. 11th Michigan Cavalry)

Dear Lizzie:

One of our patrols caught a couple of enemy deserters last night. The Rebs said they were only being paid 7 dollars a month in Confederate dollars. That isn't even enough to buy a small sack of flour because their money is worthless. They'd deserted because they were afraid their families were going to starve to death without a man around to look after their farms. It didn't seem likely that they were going to us any more harm so we let them go . . .

"Welcome home to Johnson's Island Prison, boys. Nice to have you back where you belong." Sergeant Perry Mott was in fine form. He could hardly believe his luck when it was announced the two escaped prisoners had been recaptured. It was his job to punish the ones who'd tried to escape, a task he relished. Now the two sullen Rebs were digging with shovels in the hard earth, sweat pouring off their half-naked bodies.

"Keep on digging 'til I tell you that you've gone deep enough," barked Mott. "Then you're gonna fill in the dirt and start digging in another place. Oh, we are gonna have so much fun." He hooted in glee.

Billy Bacon and Alexander Beauchine knew better than to say anything. They kept their mouths shut, tried to ignore the fresh blisters on their hands, and kept shoveling. Hopefully their torture would be short-lived. If things went according to plan they'd soon be able to take their revenge on Sergeant Mott. They'd already had a chance to explain Savard's escape plan to some of the highest-ranking officers in the prison. The officers were delighted and pledged their full support. Freedom was nearly at hand.

Bacon and Beauchine had already decided how to take their revenge on the evil Sergeant Mott. They were going to bury him alive.

"I'm ready to do the right thing, Uncle Alan."

Alan Pickle looked at his nephew with distaste, not really hearing what the young man had said. "Have you cleaned your boot out?"

Archie flushed. "Yes, I have." He'd hoped the story of his humiliation would remain secret. Apparently Mary Eliza had spilled the beans. "But that's not what I'm talking about. I want you to know that I've changed my mind about the army. I'm prepared to do my patriotic duty."

The two men were in the kitchen where Pickle was grinding coffee. George had just opened the door and was carrying in a basket of eggs. He looked up at the men, wondering if he'd interrupted something.

Pickle was delighted with his nephew. He slapped the boy on the back. "I knew you had it in you, Archie. When are you going to make the family proud of you?"

"Hopefully, right now." He turned to George. "You must be the egg boy."

"That's right." George had already heard about the young American visitor from Mary Eliza. He glanced down to see if Archie was wearing the tall black boots that she'd described.

"I understand your father joined the American army in order to collect the bounty?"

Archie's tone was disdainful and George felt his blood chill. "My father is in a Michigan cavalry regiment," he said coldly. "He's just been promoted to sergeant."

"Oh, good for him." Archie smiled insincerely. "Listen, you're a strapping big lad. I'll bet the recruiting officers wouldn't ask too many questions if you were to show up on their doorstep."

George was instantly suspicious. "What are you talking about?"

"I'm giving you the chance to see your father again soon. I'm prepared to offer you two hundred dollars if you'll act as my substitute. Of course, I'll have to get my father's approval before spending that much money. I'm quite certain he'll agree though."

Archie waited impatiently. George stood still as a statue, his face impassive. It certainly wasn't the favourable reaction Archie had been hoping for. What was the Canadian's problem? His father was nothing more than a common mercenary after all. You'd think he'd jump at the chance to make a pile of money. Archie was about to warn George that time was running out on the offer when his uncle interrupted him.

"Do you mean to say that your idea of doing your patriotic duty is to buy a replacement?" Alan Pickle was furious. He expected more courage from his relatives than he demanded of himself.

"As long as the army has a warm body to put in a uniform, what does it matter?" He turned to George. "Well, what do you say? How does two hundred dollars sound to you?"

"I believe the going price is now closer to three hundred dollars," said George dryly. "And I'd say you're a coward." He turned his back on Archie and walked away.

Archie called after him. "All right, you win. Three hundred dollars it is."

It was time to move. The last group of Confederates checked out of their hotel in Sarnia. The bill was paid in full. The innkeeper was sorry to see them go. Although the Southerners were occasionally rowdy, they were generally a good-natured bunch. They told everyone they were taking the train to Toronto. From there they were going to board ships to make their way home by sneaking through the Yankee naval blockade. The story was a lie. In reality the men had all volunteered to take part in a dangerous mission, although they didn't yet know what their assignment was.

In Toronto, a messenger went to the shabby rooming house where Frank Happa was supposedly staying. The ill-tempered landlord said he'd evicted Happa for fighting with one of the other guests. He had no idea where Happa might have gone and didn't particularly care. The messenger was exasperated. The gunslinger was definitely more trouble than he was worth. He was probably lying drunk in a bar.

For about the hundredth time, Frank Happa wished he still had his gun. The egg boy was driving his buckboard along quiet residential streets, unaware that a lone horseman was following at a discreet distance. It would have been so easy to ride up beside the buckboard, shoot, and then gallop away. By firing at point blank range, a man could be sure of hitting the target even he had to use his weak hand. Of course, you can't shoot if you don't have a gun. Happa still planned to kill the boy. It was just going to take a little extra planning.

George was deep in thought as he sat in the wagon's high seat. There was no need for him to pay attention. Winchester, the wise old horse, knew exactly where he was going. George was thinking that world was more complicated than he had ever imagined. Of all the people he'd met recently, the one he liked most was Richard Savard. But Savard was a Confederate. As such, he was the sworn enemy of everyone wearing a blue uniform, including George's father. Savard also defended the institution of slavery. Having met Bessie and her family, George had no doubts that slavery was evil.

George had secretly enjoyed the challenges of being a spy. He believed that he was helping Britain, which he'd always considered his country. Now Detective Campbell had suggested it was time to start thinking of himself as Canadian instead of British. Life isn't easy when you have deep Loyalist roots, a father in the American army and a Confederate friend.

George didn't even have to pull on the reins. Winchester automatically came to a stop outside a café. It was the last stop on his regular route. George picked up a basket of eggs and got down from the buckboard. Still deep in though, he began walking along the boardwalk. His daydream was interrupted by the unnatural sound of hoof-beats on wood.

If George had looked over his shoulder to see what the commotion was about, it may well have cost him his life. Instead, thanks to a rapidly improving survival instinct, he jumped to his left and rolled under a parked wagon. Eggs rolled from the basket and were splattered by pounding hooves. George jerked his head and saw a mounted man put the spurs to his horse. People began spilling out of the café, shouting at the crazy man who'd nearly run down a pedestrian.

Happa had failed again, though not by much. He'd watched expectantly as George stopped the buckboard and stepped down. As soon as the boy was walking along the wooden sidewalk, Happa spurred his horse forward. The well-trained animal, which had been stolen earlier in the day, obediently jumped onto the boardwalk and raced forward. If the horse had been a second faster, or the boy had been a fraction slower, history might have been changed.

Sixteen

(Excerpt of letter from Sgt. William Duguay. 11th Michigan Cavalry)

Dearest Lizzie:

Finally, victory! It took 3 days of the hardest fighting anyone has ever seen, but we beat General Lee's invincible Confederate army. It's the first time I've ever seen the Rebs run away. We've been ordered to chase the rascals all the way back to Virginia, so I suspect I'll be in the saddle for a while. I'll write as often as I can . . .

George's mother fed him a late lunch and then walked over to a neighbour's cabin to do some quilting. She didn't know about the latest attempt on her son's life. George reasoned she already had quite enough to worry about, what with his father riding after the whole Rebel army.

Although George hadn't said a word about the incident, it had left him badly shaken. It looked as if spies were in just as much danger as combat soldiers, perhaps more. He thought about quitting, mostly because there would be no one to look after his mother if something happened to him.

George was planning to work while his mother was away. He was finally getting around to replacing the rotten floor boards on one of the chicken coops. The prospect of working with his hands was pleasing. His father always said that a little sweat was the best thing to clear a mind.

While burdened with a load of lumber George heard the sound of a galloping horse. His heart fluttered like a frightened bird. Had the gunman tracked him to the farm? He dropped the boards and prepared to run.

George took a quick look over his shoulder and stopped dead in his tracks. It wasn't danger that was racing towards the farm. It was his good friend Savard.

"Sorry to drop in unannounced," said the Confederate with a broad smile. A fine horseman, he'd clearly enjoyed the gallop. "I just wanted to see you before I go."

George was surprised. "Go? Where are you headed?"

"Back home." Savard climbed down from his horse. "I'm leaving tomorrow morning. Catching a train to Montreal. From there I'll take a ship to Bermuda. Lots of blockade-runners are based there. I'll get on board one of them and sneak past the Union gunboats."

It was the answer to George's prayers. The police would no longer need him to work as a spy once Savard was gone. He could quit without fear of being branded a coward. However, he was careful not to show his elation. "I'll miss you," he said simply.

As soon as the words were out, George realized he'd been speaking the truth. Even though Savard was a Confederate, it was hard to think of him as an enemy. The man had so many qualities that it was almost impossible to dislike him.

"I'm going to miss you too." Savard draped an arm around George's shoulders and gave the boy a hug. Then he said softly, "Is your mother visiting her friend?"

At that moment George realized he'd blundered earlier by telling Savard about the quilting party. A good spy never volunteers more information than is absolutely necessary.

"She's gone," he admitted.

Savard smiled broadly. "If she doesn't know that her land has been polluted by a Rebel's footsteps, then she won't care. Is it all right if I have a last visit with you? Maybe I can help you work on that chicken coop."

"That would be nice," said George. He said a silent prayer that his mother wouldn't come home early.

"I've got some delicious sweet rolls in my saddle bags," said Savard. "Trawick's housekeeper made them. I thought you'd enjoy some. Let's put them in the house, out of the sun."

He took the saddlebags off his mare and walked towards the house. George walked beside him, not yet aware of the danger.

As soon as the door opened and Savard stepped inside, George's wits returned. "Look at that," he said loudly. He pointed at the musket hanging over the fireplace. "That's my great-grandfather's musket from the war of 1812."

Savard politely stepped forward to inspect the gun. At the same moment George hopped backwards and stood against the wall, hoping he was tall enough to block any view of the photograph. Savard made a few respectful comments about the fine condition of the old weapon, took a quick glance around the inside of the small house, and headed outside again.

George quickly turned, snatched the picture of his father from off the wall, and tossed it behind a pile of firewood. If he'd seen the picture, Savard would certainly have had a few questions about the identity of the man wearing an American uniform. Breathing heavily, George scrambled outside.

Despite the summer warmth, Savard wore a long coat. It was very fashionable and he must have been very proud of it. Or perhaps, being a southerner, he found that Canadian summers weren't hot enough for his liking. Savard walked inside the chicken coop and inspected the rotten boards that needed replacing.

"No need to get this dirty," he said, taking off the coat and hanging it from a hook on the inside of the door.

The work proceeded very quickly. Savard was skilled with his hands and wasn't afraid to work up a sweat. He was also in a good mood, cracking jokes, telling stories, and singing. Slowly George began to relax. Then he began enjoying himself. Savard was an extremely easy man to like.

When there was only one more floorboard to put in Savard turned to his young friend. "Say George, why don't you run back to the house and fetch those sweet rolls? I'll have the last board nailed in by the time you get back."

George thought it was a great idea. He put down his saw and ran to the house. By the time he returned with the snacks, Savard was hammering in the last nail. George politely lifted Savard's coat off the hook and handed it to him. They went outside, washed up, and ate the buns. Then it was time for the Confederate to take his leave.

"I don't expect I'll be seeing you again, George. At least not any time soon. I'll always think of you fondly." Savard was being perfectly genuine. He'd developed a deep affection for the quiet, young Canadian.

Savard embraced the boy, then got on his mare and rode away.

Once again George was left with conflicting emotions. There was no doubt that Savard was the most amazing person he'd ever met. He was intelligent, educated, talented and humorous. Savard was also a true patriot. How could such an admirable man defend a country that practiced slavery? It was a question that George Duguay never satisfactorily answered.

George waited for a while, just to make certain that Savard had a good head start. Then he hitched Winchester to the buckboard and headed into town. It was time to perform his last duty for Queen and Country.

Inspector Stansbury appeared to be staring at the pencil he'd been twirling in his fingers. In reality his mind was racing so fast that he was barely aware of what his hands were doing. "So Savard is leaving for Montreal in the morning, eh?"

"He said he doesn't think he's ever coming back this way," added George.

Stansbury would have agents at the main railway station just to make sure Savard really did leave. He'd heard reports from Montreal that Confederate agents were starting to turn up there. The news was very disturbing.

"I guess you won't be needing me any more." It was said as a statement, not a question.

Stansbury studied the egg boy's impassive face. It was impossible to tell if he was sad or delighted to discover that his services were no longer required. The inspector finally understood just how badly he'd underestimated the youngster. No doubt about it, George was good at masking his emotions.

"You've done well. Your talent for deception has come as a pleasant surprise to us. You've provided a valuable service to Her Majesty's government."

The boy hesitated before answering. "You aren't going to try and pay me again, are you?"

Stansbury's face betrayed the barest flicker of a smile. "No. I know better than to do that." He looked at the lad with curiosity. "Between the two of us, what was the most difficult part of the job?"

George replied instantly. "Betraying someone you like. Someone who trusts you."

The inspector nodded sympathetically. "That can be hard to get used to."

Early next morning Richard Savard caught the train to Montreal. Canadian agents kept an eye on him the entire way. Once there, however, he managed to elude his followers. It was as if he'd vanished off the face of the earth.

Life returned to normal for George Duguay. He delivered eggs, ran errands, and worked at his chores. In his heart though, he knew he'd changed forever. Mary Eliza spotted the transition right away. Every day, when he made his deliveries to the Pickford Inn, she'd make a comment about how he was turning into a man before her eyes. And she wasn't just trying to make him blush.

Seventeen

(Excerpt of letter from Major W.A. Frances, 11th Michigan Cavalry)

> *Dear Mrs. Duguay:*
>
> *It is my painful duty to inform you that I have some very sad news about your brave husband. Sergeant Duguay has officially been listed as Missing in Action . . .*

The handwriting on the envelope wasn't familiar. Lizzie Duguay opened it with a sense of dread. She read the letter several times, not understanding. Missing in action. What did that mean? Was that just a polite way of saying William was dead and that they couldn't find the body? Lizzie clutched the letter to her chest and began to cry. She should never have let her husband go off to war. No farm is worth the loss of a loved one.

News of the tragedy spread quickly through the close-knit rural community. Neighbours visited in a steady stream. The women, sad but practical, brought presents of food. They knew Lizzie wouldn't feel like cooking for quite some time.

The men, unsure of what to say, invariably patted George on the head, as if he was still a little boy. They urged him to be strong and not to give up hope. George hardly responded. He couldn't. It was as if his entire body had gone numb and he'd lost the ability to speak.

The next day was Sunday. The minister asked the congregation to pray for the safe return of Sergeant William Duguay. George sat silently, holding his mother's hand. People stole glances at him throughout the service. They noted how big he had grown over the past few months and how much he looked like his father. More than one person realized that they hardly knew George at all, although he'd lived in the area all his life. The boy was something of a loner and he kept his thoughts to himself.

George needed some private time. Lizzie understood her son's longing for solitude and raised no objections when he said he wanted to go hunting. They both knew it was just an excuse to go for a walk in the woods. He saddled Winchester and set out along the creek. The trees and shrubs offered welcome shelter from the rest of the world.

With his father's hunting musket slung over his back, George rode towards the Trawick estate. After all, the old gentleman had said he was welcome any time. There was no need to even ask for permission.

Shortly after arriving at Trawick's property George found a lovely meadow. It was a perfect spot to tie up Winchester. There was shade, water, and lots of sweet grass. George left the horse behind and headed along a path.

Although he flushed some game, he didn't shoot at it. He wasn't in the mood for hunting. It was a good thing he felt that way. The roar of the musket would have attracted unwelcome attention.

George soon came to the edge of the woods where he had a clear view of Trawick's house and barns. It certainly wasn't as quiet as the last time he'd been there. Several dozen men had set up camp. Some were helping load heavy boxes onto wagons. Others napped under trees, played cards, or gathered in small groups to gossip.

Some of the men seemed to be standing guard. They were posted in pairs near the entrance to the farm and at the manor house itself. Only the guards were armed. Long lines of horses were saddled, ready for instant action. Although he'd never seen a military camp before, George knew instinctively that these men were soldiers. He could hear snatches of conversation. The accents weren't local.

George left the musket leaning against an elm tree. It was longer than George was tall. It would have been difficult to crawl silently through the grass and brush while carrying the musket.

He noticed three men sitting on a rail fence, chewing tobacco. Their backs were towards George. He pulled himself forward on his elbows until he could clearly hear what they were saying.

The men were discussing the merits of some sort of military operation. Their officers had only given them the details a few minutes ago. Now they were debating the plan's strengths and weaknesses. Generally they liked what they'd been told.

George listened to the conversation with a growing sense of anxiety. He quickly realized that all of the men were escaped Confederate prisoners who had banded together. They were going to ride into Toronto and take over an American passenger steamer. Some of the Rebels were already aboard the ship, disguised as ordinary passengers. At a preset time, they were to take the captain and crew hostage. The rest of the secret army would then board the ship, and sail as quickly as possible to the American side of the lake.

The ship's destination was Johnson's Island, the Union prison camp. Nearly three thousand Southern captives were held there. They'd already been told a raiding party was on the way to free them and supply weapons. The prisoners of Johnson's Island would form a new Confederate army in the heart of enemy territory.

The raiding party was supposed to burn Sandusky, the town across the harbour from the prison. Then the guerillas would get back on the ship and sail to Buffalo, New York. That city would also be set ablaze. After causing as much mischief as possible the raiders would retreat to Canada. It was hoped that an outraged American government would send troops into Canada to try and capture the raiders. An armed invasion of one of her colonies was certain to bring Britain into the war. The Confederacy would finally have the strong ally it needed.

Something strange happened to George. He'd been lethargic and depressed since the news about his father arrived. Now, as he listened to the men talk, his senses came alive. The brain began working again. He knew his country needed him once more. It was enough to get him out of his funk.

"Them Yanks are gonna get the shock of their lives," said a husky man wearing a battered felt hat. He chuckled loudly.

"Look, here comes Savard," said one of his companions. "It's about time."

George raised his head ever so slightly and peered through some branches. The man who had mentioned Savard's name was standing up, massaging a stiff shoulder. He looked vaguely familiar.

Savard came into view. "I heard you were looking for me, Happa." There was an edge to his voice. Happa had arrived late at the camp. Since then he'd been demanding to see Savard, saying he had important information.

"In private, if ya please."

The other two men were dismissed. Savard looked at Happa with distaste. He couldn't stomach the murderous ruffian. "Well, what's on your mind?"

Happa grinned, displaying a mouth of rotting teeth. "It's about this kid I keep runnin' into. I think you know him pretty well. He delivers eggs."

"You must be referring to George. Yes, I know him. He's a friend of mine."

"Then ya need new friends," Happa said tersely. "He works fer the British, and probably fer the Yanks as well. I seen him go inside the police station with a Canadian detective. He stayed a long time. Then I seen him at your old boarding house. He asked fer you. Your landlady said you and the boy have been spendin' a lot of time together. My guess is everything you say to him is passed on to the police." What he didn't say was that the landlady had innocently told him where George lived.

There was a sinking feeling in Savard's stomach, but he didn't let it show. "That doesn't prove anything," he growled. "Even if what you say is true, which I highly doubt."

"Doubt all you want," said Happa. He moved in for the kill. "But I've been askin' around about the boy. I bet he didn't tell you his pa is in the Union army. Ha! I can tell by your face that you didn't know. It's true!" He chortled in triumph.

Savard was horrified. Had he really been outsmarted by a boy? He didn't know what felt worse, the sense of betrayal or the fear that George had discovered the plan. Should the raid be cancelled? Savard thought about it for a moment and his confidence returned. He was positive he'd never let any information about the secret mission slip out. George couldn't possibly know anything about it.

Happa was growing weary of waiting for a response. "Somethin' has to be done about that boy," he said. "He's wrecked the plan. You can't go ahead now."

"Forget the boy!" snapped Savard. "That's an order. He doesn't know a thing about the plan. There's no need to cancel anything. The British won't have a clue that anything is amiss until an American army crosses into Canada ."

Happa noisily spat on the ground. "Sure," he said. "You're the boss." He didn't say it like he meant it. To his way of thinking he'd tried to do his countrymen a favour by telling them the plan may have been discovered. If they wanted to go ahead anyway there was nothing he could do about it. Not that he'd ever had any intention of joining the raid.

Savard strode away, glad he'd confiscated the gunslinger's weapons earlier. It would be just like Happa to do something crazy if he were armed.

In fact, hidden underneath a long coat, Happa was carrying a brand new pistol. Jacob Thompson had presented it to him the previous day. The jealous Confederate spymaster wanted to know what his rival was up to. Happa was only too willing to help, for a promise of money and a new gun.

As soon as Happa had learned the details of the raid he was supposed to ride straight to the Royal Roads hotel. Thompson was there, anxiously waiting for information. It was going to be a very profitable day for Happa. But first he had a stop to make. He hadn't told anyone that he'd tried again to kill the boy and failed. It was embarrassing to admit defeat. He had a score to settle.

George had heard every word of the conversation between Happa and his former friend. He watched the gunslinger casually walk towards the horses. Then he ran a short distance into the woods. There, behind a giant oak tree, he was violently ill.

Eighteen

(Excerpt of letter from Lt. Nathaniel Plummer, 11th Michigan Calvary)

Dear Mrs. Duguay:

I have the honour of being your husband's commanding officer. He fought heroically at my side when our troop was ambushed by Confederate cavalry. During the fight Sgt. Duguay was wounded, but insisted upon staying behind to cover our retreat.

We have now been informed by the Confederates that your husband was captured and is being held prisoner. Until recently there were regular prisoner exchanges between the two armies. Sadly, they were discontinued because the Rebels are furious with the Union for using Negro soldiers . . .

George knew he was in grave danger. If the Confederates caught him, he'd probably be shot. He grabbed the musket and ran to the clearing where Winchester was grazing. It was some distance and it took George half an hour to get there, a dangerously long time. There was no time to saddle up. George grabbed the startled horse, slipped on the bridle, and rode bareback.

George had to get home as quickly as possible and warn his mother. The Confederates were about to break camp and head for Toronto. If Savard was looking for revenge, he could make a short detour and visit the Duguay farm. He didn't yet understand that the greatest risk came from someone other than Savard.

As soon as he was out of Savard's view, Frank Happa strolled over to where the horses were tied up. He picked out a big bay and slapped its rump. "I saw this one limping earlier," Happa lied to the guard.

He took a knife out of its sheath, lifted one of the horse's legs and pretended to examine a hoof. Then he poked at the horseshoe with the blade of his knife. "There's a rock in there. No wonder he was gimpy. I think I got it out. Maybe I should take him for a trot 'round the farm, just to make sure everything is okay. We don't want him pullin' up lame when it's time to move out."

The bored guard nodded his approval.

Happa mounted the animal and casually rode off. When he was out of the guard's view he changed direction and cantered to the main road. With luck nobody would notice his absence until it was too late. After riding for a while, Happa came to a fork in the road. He slowed down, checked one last time to make certain he had no pursuers, and made a decision.

He could have taken the route that led directly to Toronto. Instead he turned off the main road. The gunslinger was headed for the Duguay farm. He'd taken the time to find out where that meddling egg boy lived. This time there would be no mistakes.

To his great relief, Archie Chittendon was going home to New York City. The trip to Canada had been a total disaster. It was bad enough that Uncle Alan wanted him to join the Union army, but worse, the American agents staying at the inn had threatened to hang him for treason. The only safe and sensible thing was to get out of Toronto as quickly as possible. Luckily he had been able to book passage on a fine steamship. The 'Island Queen' would soon be sailing back to the United States.

Adding to his good humour, Archie had just made a new acquaintance. By coincidence, a veteran Mississippi paddle-wheel captain was also on board the ship. Captain Bates stood by the rail of the ship, watched every passenger who came aboard, and chatted amiably to Archie before excusing himself. To keep himself amused, the young American began imitating the captain's southern accent.

George won the race to his farm. He'd taken the path along the creek. Although it was rougher than the road, it was also considerably shorter.

Lizzie Duguay was outside, throwing scraps of bread to a flock of squawking chickens. She stopped and watched in amazement as her son galloped up. He was soaked in sweat and the front of his shirt was stained.

"Run to the McCandless house as fast as you can," shouted George. "There's a secret Confederate army just a few miles away. They're trying to start a war between Britain and America. They just found out that I've been helping the police. Some of the

Rebs may come here to look for me. You must leave right now. I have to ride into town to spread the alarm."

A dozen questions flooded Lizzie's mind. She never got the chance to ask a single one. George slammed his heels into the horse's flanks and sped off. His mother watched him disappear around the corner of the road. Then, reluctantly, she went to the cabin.

George lashed at Winchester's neck with the reins, urging him to go faster. Although the horse was past his prime, he was still game. He also sensed his young master's urgency. Winchester stretched his long legs to run the race of his life.

Lizzie took a pot of stew off the wood stove. For a woman who'd been told to run for her life it seemed an odd thing to do. Always practical, however, Lizzie knew the stew could start a fire if it were left to boil away until all the liquid was gone. After all, she had no idea when it might be safe to return.

George had been giving sensible advice when he told her to go to the McCandless house. He was a former fur trader with three teenage sons. All of them were deadly shots. She would be as safe there as anywhere.

Reluctantly, Lizzie headed towards the door. The rough cabin contained nearly everything her family owned. What if the Confederates came and set it on fire? War had devastated her family twice before. Now there was a risk of it happening again.

As she stood in the doorway Lizzie caught saw a horse and rider appear out of a nearby grove of trees. Her chances of escaping were now very poor. She watched and listened for a moment, then made up her mind.

It was the right farm, no doubt about it. Everything matched the description Frank Happa had been given, from the unpainted house to the ramshackle chicken coops. Smoke drifted out of the chimney, indicating someone was home. Happa sniffed the air, catching a whiff of cooking meat. Judging from the savoury scent, the boy's mother knew how to cook. He wondered if she was pretty as well.

Happa didn't ride up the drive. That would have made it too easy to spot him. There was a thicket of trees not far from the house. He led the bay there and tied it to a sapling. Then Happa took the new pistol from his belt and rejoiced in the feel of it. He regretted there hadn't been more time to practice shooting with his wrong hand.

Ducking from tree to tree, Happa approached the farm. He didn't want to get too close to the chicken coops. The birds could be notoriously noisy if a stranger ventured too near. The gunman stopped for a moment and searched the farmyard. There was no human movement at all. That made sense. The boy was probably inside the house with his mother. Well they were about to have some unexpected company for supper.

Happa sprinted to a large pile of firewood next to the outhouse. He pulled back the hammer of his revolver to prepare it for firing. Something moved to his left. A figure stepped from behind a small shed. Instinctively, he turned and fired.

Elizabeth Ann MacDavid Duguay had a heart as stout as any soldier's. She barely flinched as the bullet nicked her waist. Lizzie had fired muskets many times as a girl, beating her brothers in competition more times than they'd like to admit. Her grandfather's ancient musket roared and an enormous cloud of black smoke billowed into the air.

Happa had been shot before. In his last battle, an arm had nearly been torn off by a Yankee bullet. That time, despite the severity of the wound, he'd still been able to think and fight and curse. This time he was on his back, unable to move. A woman leaned over him, examined him carefully, and then stepped back. She expertly reloaded the musket. There was no need to hurry. The fight was finished.

"I'm done for." There was surprise in Happa's voice.

"So you are," said Lizzie calmly. Then she turned and walked away. Her own wound was a mere scratch.

Lizzie figured the intruder she'd just shot was a solitary scout. Other Confederates might be near. There was no way a single woman could hold off a group of trained soldiers. It was time to take refuge with the neighbours, even if it meant her farm was going to be burnt.

Canadian militiamen ran from house to house, excitedly calling for their friends and neighbours to report for duty. Redcoats marched from their camp under the watchful eyes of officers. Police officers listened wide-eyed to their orders and then raced off. In the midst of all the commotion a very calm British major turned to the young spy he'd just met for the first time.

"I'd appreciate it if you'd act as guide," he said. "I understand you know the country well. Besides, you'll be able to identify this Savard chap. I definitely want to question him." He looked skeptically at Winchester. The ancient creature was on the verge of collapse after his marathon run. "We'll get you a fresh horse."

The major noted with surprise that the spy was really just a boy. Still, the lad was blessed with both courage and wits. He might make a fine soldier some day.

Nineteen

(Excerpt of letter from Sgt. William Duguay, 11th Michigan Cavalry)

> *Darling Lizzie:*
>
> *I don't know if, or when, you will ever get this letter. I am being held by the Confederates at Andersonville Prison. Now I know what Hell is like. The guards are deliberately starving us. Dozens of prisoners die, or are murdered, every day . . .*

None of the Confederates were armed. Their orders specified that nobody could carry weapons until they were actually on board the ship. All of the escaped prisoners were combat veterans. If they had guns and were confronted by the police, they'd be certain to open fire. Their leader knew the British and Canadians would be furious if any of their people were killed or wounded in a gunfight. It was better to surrender meekly than hurt a single Receipt. The last thing Richard Savard wanted was to annoy the people he wanted as allies.

Three large wagons left the Trawick estate. They were loaded with crates labeled Shovels or Nails. In reality the wooden boxes were filled with guns and ammunition. The drivers had orders to go directly to Toronto harbour. Confederate agents posing as businessmen had booked cargo space on board the steamer Island Queen. The crew thought an ordinary shipment of hardware was coming aboard. By the time they found out what was really inside the boxes, it would be too late.

"How y'all doin'?" said Archie Chittendon in a low voice. Nobody paid him the slightest attention. He lounged along the rail of the ship, practicing southern accents. "I's from No' Carolinah. Whar y'all from?"

Archie ignored the burly men moving heavy crates off some recently arrived wagons. "Yo sure is a purty gal," chirped Archie. He was so busy daydreaming of sweeping pretty girls off their feet that he didn't notice what was happening at the wharf.

A gang of uniformed police officers had silently made their way through the piles of cargo and surrounded the wagons. Taken totally by surprise, the astonished wagon crews surrendered without a fight.

Satisfied that his men were in control of the docks, Detective Campbell trotted up the ship's gangplank. A dozen armed policemen followed. They were all dressed in civilian clothes. Campbell noticed a young man standing near the stern. He appeared to be talking to himself.

The detective approached cautiously, a hand on the revolver hidden inside his coat. Archie heard footsteps and looked up. He smiled at the newcomer. It seemed like a perfect opportunity to see if he could pass for a Southern gentleman.

"How y'all doin?" he asked. "Purty day, ain't it?"

"A very pretty day indeed," replied Campbell. "You sound like you're from the Deep South, if I'm not mistaken."

"No, you ain't mistook," said Archie. He was delighted that his little joke was working so well.

Campbell was also pleased. Through sheer good luck he'd stumbled upon one of the Confederate agents who were preparing to take over the ship. He took the pistol out from under his coat and stuck the barrel into Archie's open mouth. "Don't make a sound, Reb," growled Campbell. "You are in a world of trouble."

Archie wasn't given the opportunity to explain who he really was. As soon as the gun barrel was pulled from his mouth a dirty handkerchief was shoved in. His hands and feet were tightly bound and he was tossed into a cargo net. Then Campbell raced off to help his men secure the rest of the ship.

It would be another two days before Archie Chittendon was able to convince the Canadian police that he was an innocent passenger. Although Uncle Alan was humiliated beyond belief by his nephew's latest show of stupidity, he helped the boy gain his freedom. Archie eventually made it back to New York City, where he was arrested for evading the draft.

The blisters on his hands had burst open. The pain was so great that Billy Bacon could barely keep on shovelling. Sergeant Perry Mott noticed Bacon's discomfort and shouted an insult. Bacon just smiled, knowing the prisoners of Johnson's Island were scheduled be set free by the next evening. Mott would pay for his bullying after the daring raid. Bacon glanced towards the lake, praying that the ship carrying his countrymen would arrive soon. He didn't know how much more abuse he could take.

The wagon trundled through pleasant countryside. Two men sat on the seat. They looked exactly like farmers on the way into town. What the casual onlooker wouldn't have realized is that a dozen men were lying under canvas tarps in the back of the wagon. They'd stay hidden until the wagon reached the harbour.

The driver suddenly swore and pulled up on the reins. Two men had jumped up from their hiding place in the ditch. Their muskets were pointed at the driver and his companion.

"Bushwhackers!" groaned the driver. He couldn't believe his bad luck. What a time to be robbed. But then another two armed men walked out of the brush — Canadian militiamen who had been called out so quickly they didn't have time to put on their uniforms.

A group of mounted Redcoats galloped up. "You are all under arrest," shouted a young lieutenant. His voice was squeaking with excitement. "And that includes everyone hiding under the canvas." He leaned from his horse and slashed at the tarp with a riding crop. The man he'd hit yelped in pain, then stuck his head out and blinked in the sunlight.

"Hold on, Jones," snapped a captain with huge sideburns. "That wasn't very sporting. Don't hit the scoundrels unless they try and run away."

The lieutenant blushed and said he was sorry. Then to the astonishment of all the Confederates, the young officer apologized to the prisoner he'd struck.

Happa had deserted. There was no longer any doubt about it. Savard feared the worst when he heard the gunslinger had disappeared with one of the horses. It was possible that he'd simply decided he wanted no part of the upcoming battles and run away. It was just as possible that he was in the pay of the Canadians, the Americans, or even Thompson's spy group.

Savard took a horse and went in the direction Happa had ridden. It was possible the bay really had gone lame and Happa was walking back to the farm. After he scouted along the edge of the woods and saw no sign of a horseman, Savard knew in his heart the ruffian had bolted.

It seemed unlikely the expedition could be kept secret for much longer. There was no time to waste. The ammunition wagons had left the farm hours ago, followed a short time later by the first wagonload of men. The remaining men were lounging near the horses, waiting for their orders. The original plan had called for them to leave in two groups when it got dark, so as not to attract attention. Savard decided to get the remaining men moving right away.

It was an order he never got the chance to give. Scarlet horsemen were pouring into the farmyard, waving sabres. British cavalry! Most of the unarmed Confederates simply surrendered. A few turned and ran towards the thick woods at the opposite end of the farm. They ran straight of the arms of the Canadian militiamen who were waiting with loaded muskets.

It was as efficient as any ambush Savard had ever witnessed. The raid had turned into a shambles. However, fortune had placed him a considerable distance from the action. He turned his horse and rode, unseen, into the trees. It was time to save himself.

"He's not here." George had inspected every one of the Confederate prisoners. "Savard must have escaped."

"Well he won't get far," vowed the gruff cavalry captain. "He'll probably head south, towards the Sarnia crossing. But just to be sure, we'll have men at every train station in Upper Canada."

George thought for a moment. Then he climbed back onto the horse the army had lent him. Nobody paid the slightest attention. As far as the soldiers were concerned, he was just a local guide whose job was done.

Savard had a general idea of where he was going, although he'd never taken the backwoods route. He moved slowly along the creek, trying to stay on the narrow path. It was getting dark and he didn't want the horse to stumble and hurt itself. Savard regretted that he'd tried to set an example for his men by not carrying a gun. Oh, well. He'd remedy that soon enough.

Twenty

Richard Savard felt a sense of dread as he rode closer to the Duguay farm. Something was amiss. There was no sign of human activity. The front door of the cabin swung in the breeze. No candles or lanterns burned inside. Chickens wandered the farmyard in the dusk. They should have been locked in their coops for the night, safe from foxes and owls.

Savard shuddered at the thought of what had likely happened. Happa must have been there already. That would explain the unnatural quiet. Savard felt a deep sense of betrayal against George. Still, he hoped the boy and his mother hadn't suffered too much at the hands of the traitor.

There didn't seem to be any need for secrecy. It was unlikely anyone was still alive to see him. Savard rode straight to the chicken coop he'd helped repair. A few of the hens squawked accusingly as they darted out of the horse's path.

Savard went into the coop and found the floorboard he'd personally installed. He pried at it with a knife. The board should have been nailed tight, but it lifted without effort. Savard was stunned. His hiding place had been discovered. The hollow space under the flooring was empty. His package was gone! An already disastrous day had turned even worse.

The Confederate's brain was swirling. He was now a fugitive with nothing to his name but a horse and the clothes on his back. There wasn't much chance of escaping from Canada unless he also managed to get his hands on food, money and a weapon. Savard wondered if Happa had taken the time to loot the cabin. Perhaps there was some food left inside. If he was very lucky, the old musket might still be hanging on the wall.

Going into the cabin wouldn't be pleasant. There were probably bodies inside. Still, Savard was no stranger to death. He stepped outside the chicken coop.

"Are you looking for this?" George stood a few paces away, holding tightly onto a revolver with both hands. Savard immediately recognized the pistol. It was the one he'd hidden in the coop. The gun was cocked, ready to fire.

"That sure was a hot day when you helped me fix the floor in the chicken coop," George continued. "I was curious why you were wearing heavy clothes. When you sent me to the house for the sticky buns, I accidentally brushed against the coat. It seemed very lumpy. Later, when I handed the coat to you, the lump was gone. It got me thinking about why you were so determined to help me fix the coop."

Savard stood rock-still, judging the distance between him and the boy. "So you figured out where I hid my emergency gear. Bully for you." There was bitterness in his voice. "You betrayed me, George."

The youngster shook his head. "No more than you betrayed me. When I was guiding you around the city you never mentioned that you were trying to start a war."

"I was just doing my patriotic duty," said Savard quietly. He took a tiny step forward.

"And I'm just doing mine," replied George. His was pointing the gun straight at his friend. "Don't try and rush me."

Savard remained calm. "You'll have to kill me George. I can't let you take me prisoner. The British will just hang me anyway." He reached out a hand. "Give me the gun George. You know you don't want to shoot me."

Flame erupted from the barrel of the pistol. A bullet smashed into the wooden wall of the chicken coop, projecting splinters onto Savard's hat. The man jumped back involuntarily. He shook his head to clear away the echoing roar, amazed that he was still alive.

"You're partly right," said George. "I don't *want* to shoot you. I will if I have to though." He paused, looking for the right words. "What I really want to do is make a deal."

Hope flooded through Savard. Maybe he wasn't beat yet. "What sort of deal?"

"My father is in the Union army. His name is Sergeant William Duguay of the 11th Michigan Cavalry. He was wounded and taken prisoner. I want him set free."

"They've stopped the prisoner exchanges," said Savard. "It's the Yankee's fault for trying to turn niggers into soldiers. The Confederacy is prepared to start the exchanges again as soon as the Americans come to their senses."

"I'm glad to hear your government would like to start swapping prisoners again. Maybe I can get the ball rolling. I propose to trade you for my father. Do you think your bosses will trade a simple Union sergeant for one of its top spies? Answer me truthfully."

"I think it's fair to say that my government considers me to be a person of some importance," replied Savard. "I'm quite certain they'd agree to the trade."

"Will you ask them to approve the deal? Can I trust you?"

"The answer to both questions is 'yes.'"

There was a small metal box on the ground, next to George's feet. He picked it up and tossed it to Savard. "Here's the money you hid in the chicken coop. It's all there. Use it to get back to the Confederacy. Then free my father."

Savard easily caught the box in one hand. "What about the gun?" The pistol had been hidden under the floorboards along with the cash.

"I'll keep it. If you end up shooting someone on Canadian soil, I'll feel responsible. Tell you what, though. You can have another horse. That way you'll be able to cover a lot more ground. When one gets tired you can switch to the other."

Savard shook his head. "I don't want to take old Winchester from you, George."

"I'd never give up Winchester," said George firmly. "I'm offering the bay gelding the gunman stole from you earlier. It's tied up in that grove of trees over there."

"You have Happa's horse? What happened to him?"

"He's over by the woodpile. I'm going to bury him as soon as you're gone. Nobody will ever know he was here."

"Did you get him?"

"No, I just found the body," said George. "It must have been my ma."

Savard nodded approvingly. "Happa had the heart of a rattlesnake, and we all know what happens when rattlers come up against a Canadian lady." The Confederate was quiet for a moment. "I ordered him to leave your family alone," he finally said. "I swear it's true."

"I believe you," said George, remembering the conversation he'd overheard at the farm. "That's why I'm trusting that you'll keep your word and send my father home."

Savard walked to his horse and mounted it. Then he turned to the youngster who'd befriended and then outsmarted him.

"It's very easy to underestimate you, George Duguay. I don't think anyone really knows what goes on inside that mind of yours. I wish we were on the same side."

George laughed bitterly. "At first I thought spying was a game. Now I know how nasty it really is." He lowered the gun, pointing it at the ground. "The British think you'll be heading south, so I'd go east if I were you. If you can make it back to Montreal, you'll probably be fine."

There was nothing else to be said. Savard got on his horse and rode to the grove of trees where Happa's gelding was tied.

"I'm free! I'm free!" he sang to himself. "I've got two good horses, lots of money, and I know where they'll be looking for me."

Savard took the bay's reins and led him onto the road. His confidence was returning. The plan wasn't dead yet. He could start all over again in Montreal. There were lots of Confederate citizens there. As he rode past the Duguay farm he saw a familiar figure standing guard in the shadows. On impulse he stopped and called out. "I wish we were allies, George. But if I ever see you again I'll have to kill you. I'll feel bad about it, of course."

The voice that replied was clear and strong. "Just make sure you keep your word, Savard. Send my pa home, or I'll make sure you feel even worse."

A Rebel yell pierced the night. It was Savard's way of saying that he recognized, and honoured, spirit in an opponent. The Confederate saluted, spurred his horse, and was gone.

When George had fled the Confederate encampment and raced home he half-expected to find that the farm had been set on fire. Instead, everything was perfectly peaceful. Fortunately his mother was gone, meaning she must have escaped. George had breathed a huge sigh of relief.

Then he stumbled across Happa's body. George felt terribly guilty. Not because of what had happened to the man, but because of what had nearly happened to his mother. It could only have been Lizzie Duguay who'd shot the intruder. She'd surely done it in self-defence. Happa must have arrived at the farm shortly after George had warned his mother to flee. It could have just as easily been his mother's body lying on the ground.

George retrieved the gun and money from the chicken coop, climbed a tree near the road, and waited. A short while later he saw an approaching rider and recognized Savard. George understood that he'd put his mother in grave danger. It was time to make amends. The best way to do that was to gain his father's freedom.

George buried Happa under a young willow tree. It was a nicer gravesite than the murderous traitor deserved. There was a lot on the young man's mind as he dug the hole. Over the last few hours his mother had been forced to fight for her life, a dangerous spy ring had been crushed, and war had been averted.

It had been a huge gamble to let Savard escape. Inspector Stansbury would be furious if he ever found out. Still, it was a risk George felt he had to take. The Confederate considered himself a man of honour. He was likely to keep his part of the deal. If he did, all of the danger and treachery George had faced over the past few weeks would have been worth it.

But what if Savard acted out of vengeance? What if he didn't arrange for Sgt. Duguay's release? George stopped shoveling for a moment and thought about what he would do then. "It's simple," he said aloud. "I'll go get pa and bring him home. Even if it means I have to go all the way to the Confederate States of America. I'll tell the politicians that one of their spies made a deal and they should keep it."

Determination flowed through George's veins as he resumed shovelling. One way or another, his father would be freed.

(Excerpt of letter from Sgt. William Duguay. 11th Michigan Cavalry)

My Dearest Lizzie:

I have just been given the most astonishing news. I am being freed in exchange for a Confederate who was caught spying. This is a huge surprise, as there are no longer supposed to be any prisoner exchanges. Apparently I am an exception, although I can not imagine why. All I have to do is swear an oath that I will not take up arms against the Confederacy again. (Which I am perfectly willing to do.) Tell George that his father is coming home. I'm certain he will be amazed . . .

ABOUT THE AUTHOR

BARRY MCDIVITT spent twenty years in the field of journalism and his award-winning work appeared on the CBC and Global networks as well as many newspapers and magazines. McDivitt is a Writer/Producer for Global Television, living in Kelowna, BC.